goodbye to thEU

machine

Volume 1

September 2013 ~ November 2014

HUGO JENKS

www.brontovox.co.uk

www.lulu.com

Cover image:
Inspired by *Welcome to the machine* video by Pink Floyd.

First published 2014 by

Brontovox Publications

www.brontovox.co.uk

Contents

1. Introduction

We are stuck in a machine. Many of us had no opportunity to vote for it or against it.

There is a rather strange Stockholm-like syndrome which afflicts those who are enthusiastic about our membership of the European Union. Almost no evidence presented to them will convince them that we are imprisoned by this machine. The brainwashing has been expertly applied.

To undo years of brainwashing and misinformation requires a supreme effort of willpower and persistence. Fortunately we already have over 40,000 people in the UK who have seen what has happened, and are active in the effort to extract ourselves.

Freedom, true democracy, and our own laws made in our own parliament by our own elected representatives are what we so desperately need.

I do have a strong sense that our ancestors are calling out to us from across the millennia, not to abandon the birthright which we have inherited from them, and for which they have made extreme sacrifices.

We must pass on to our heirs, our children and our grandchildren the freedoms which we shall regain. It is our duty to do so.

Hugo Jenks

2. The squeeze on rents and wages

To: Bath Chronicle

Two recent letters have highlighted the pressures that all too many of us are struggling with. Affordability of housing in the Bath area was raised by Victor da Cunha (Bath Chronicle September 5) and the increasing demand on food banks was described by Jo McCarron (Bath Chronicle August 29). This is also a problem elsewhere. I have relatives in Shropshire and in the West Midlands who volunteer at food banks, and the demand is increasing there also.

We must understand the underlying causes if we have any expectation of improving these problems. Professor of economics Tim Congdon has shown that since 2004 when our borders were opened to people arriving from the A8 group of EU countries, employment for UK-born workers has declined by half a million, whilst employment for non-UK born workers has increased by nearly two million. This inevitably has put downward pressure on wages and at the same time has increased the cost of renting due to the increased demand. The human cost of this is significant.

The situation is not likely to improve, as even more workers will have the right to enter the UK from January 2014 from recent member countries of the EU. We should either put tighter limits on the numbers arriving, or be prepared to increase the size of the housing stock in line with the population increase, which between the 2001 and 2011 censuses increased by 6.9%. Can Bath really be expected to expand by this percentage every decade?

3. Food farms not solar farms

To: Western Daily Press

Solar farms are cropping up like mushrooms in many areas. The latest proposal is for 17-hectares of PV panels near Chippenham. (Western Daily Press September 7).

My primary concern is that these are taking agricultural land out of production. The UK population has increased by 6.9% in a decade (2001 to 2011 censuses) and is continuing to increase. Where will the food come from to feed all these extra mouths? We can ill afford to lose any agricultural land.

Due to poor forward planning and also due to emissions reduction targets, we are at significantly increased risk of electricity blackouts in the coming years. Most nuclear power stations are near the end of their life, coal-fired power stations are being shut down to comply with EU emission reduction requirements. In April we were close to running out of gas. The highest risk and impact of blackouts would be during the winter months, when the output from solar photovoltaic panels would be at a minimum anyway.

PV panels should be sited on steep south facing slopes, where arable crops cannot be grown.

We must urgently put in place some common sense energy policies, before we have blackouts. The elderly and vulnerable are particularly at risk if these happen during the winter, as is most probable.

4. Labour energy policy

To: Somerset Guardian

The Labour candidate for North East Somerset has written that voters have a choice of energy policies (Somerset Guardian 21 November).

Labour have already demonstrated that they cannot be trusted regarding our energy supply. The margin between generating capacity and peak demand is slim, and is becoming slimmer. Load shedding of large industrial users will limit the number of blackouts suffered by residential consumers, but at what cost to the economy and jobs?

Ed Miliband was the Energy Minister in the Labour government. During 13 years in office, Labour failed to start building any new nuclear power stations. It takes about a decade to build one, in the next decade all but one nuclear power station will come to the end of their operational life. Regarding coal, Ed Miliband and Gordon Brown have committed us to an 80% CO_2 reduction by 2050. This and the EU are obliging us to phase out coal power stations. Where are we going to get power from? Solar and wind are intermittent. In April 2013 we came close to running out of gas.

Ed Miliband wants a price freeze. Let us hope that we do not literally freeze if the lights go out. The electricity supply system is in a precarious state largely due to his decisions when in office.

5. Child Contact Centre

To: Bath Chronicle

Congratulations to Linda Wyon for being awarded an OBE. She founded the Bath Child Contact Centre in 1991.

Contact Centres are so vitally important, to allow usually the father to have time with his child. I know this from first hand experience as my own marriage failed. The Contact Centre where I then lived was brilliant, well organised and the volunteer staff helpful and understanding. I have much to thank them for. All too many children do lose contact with their father, and this is harmful both for the children and for him. It is well researched that children without their father in their life do less well, have a higher risk of criminal activity and drug taking, for girls a higher risk of teenage pregnancy.

How can the BANES Council not find the relatively modest sum of £8,500 per annum to support such an important service? The Council is dominated by the Liberal Democrats Party. The slogans of the Liberal Democrats during the last General Election included: 'a fair chance for every child' and 'no more broken promises'. Do they really have no concept of how important the Child Contact Centre is?

6. Rees-Mogg blew it

To: Western Daily Press

I had hoped that Jacob Rees-Mogg would be a breath of fresh air as an MP. Unfortunately he blew it, due to his inconsistent message regarding housing developments.

Spot the difference between his quotes. The second one relates to the proposed development in Hinton Blewett, applied for by his own mother.

'The application to build 100 houses on greenbelt land in Saltford is worrying, not only because of the disruption and overcrowding it would likely cause to the village of Saltford and its community but also because of the precedent it would set for future applications around the constituency. I am concerned that if this application were approved, it would encourage other developers to seek to build on greenbelt land in the area.' (His own website)

"Planning is a matter for the local council and is not something that an MP has any say over." (Western Daily Press January 4, 2014)

Unfortunately there is an urgent need for more housing. This Government has not been able to stop the arrivals from Europe. Building more and more housing for all these extra people is like mopping the floor frantically whilst the pipe is burst. You can never keep up, the floor will never be dry. What you have to do as the first priority is to mend the pipe.

7. Vince Cable has tied himself in knots

To: Western Daily Press

Vince Cable has written to oppose the rise of UKIP in his article 'Why Britain needs to stop Ukip's right-wing agenda' (WDP 14 Feb)

He is the is Secretary of State for Business, Innovation and Skills and Lib Dem MP for Twickenham. With these credentials we would hope that he had sound judgement, however he undervalued the Royal Mail share selloff, costing the taxpayer £millions. Can we trust his judgement?

I would seriously question most of what he has written in his article. For example, the myth of 3 million jobs at stake if we leave the EU. Do you suppose for a moment that the EU would place tariffs on goods that we buy from the continent, given that they sell more goods to us than we sell to them? This idea of 3 million jobs lost has to be nonsense, the source of which has its origins in an academic paper published by South Bank University in the year 2000. Prof Ian Begg, one of the authors of this work has subsequently stated: "It's always been a bit of a false perspective to say that three million jobs would be lost."

The reality is that since 2004 when the EU A8 countries joined (Poland etc.), the number of jobs for British workers has declined by about half a million while the non-British worker jobs increased by about 2 million. If the EU is so wonderful for jobs how is it that there is so much youth unemployment in the UK, and also in Greece, Spain etc? The Ford Transit van factory in Southampton has already relocated to Turkey, if the EU is so wonderful why did it not relocate to an EU country? Turkey is not in the EU. Vince Cable is not making much sense when you look at the facts dispassionately.

8. Vince Cable has welcomed immigration

To: Western Daily Press

Liberal Democrat MP Vince Cable is delighted that net migration into the UK has increased to 212,000. Unfortunately for him and for his party around 80% of the electorate are worried about excessive immigration. We simply do not have the infrastructure to cope. We have a housing crisis already, where will all these extra people live?

Many of these additional people are coming from Italy, Greece and Spain. If the EU is so wonderful for jobs, why is it that those countries are in decline? The fact that their younger and more mobile workers are coming to the UK indicates that the EU experiment is a failure. The Liberal Democrats do not make sense, they need to have the decency to admit it when they are mistaken. Fortunately the electorate can see that they have a lack of common sense, and there will soon be a significant reduction in the number of Lib Dem MEPs.

References:

http://www.libdemvoice.org/my-favourite-vince-cable-quote-on-tory-immigration-policy-38370.html

http://www.westerndailypress.co.uk/Cable-rules-cap-immigration/story-20355102-detail/story.html

9. Cameron culpability in Ukraine

To: Western Daily Press
To: Daily Telegraph

Does David Cameron bear some responsibility for the splintering of Ukraine?

In July 2013 he visited Kazakhstan and said: "Britain has always supported the widening of the EU. Our vision of the EU is that it should be a large trading and co-operating organisation that effectively stretches, as it were, from the Atlantic to the Urals." This of course means that Cameron wants Ukraine to join the EU. The interesting question is then, where did this policy originate? Is Cameron acting alone or is he under instructions?

In October 2012 in a joint communication by Hillary Clinton and Baroness Ashton they stated: 'The European Union and Ukraine have completed negotiations on an ambitious Association Agreement that will provide for the country's political association and economic integration with the European Union..'

Baroness Ashton is the High Representative of the European Union for foreign affairs and security policy. David Cameron needs to be extremely cautious, and stop antagonising Russia. He should put the interests of Britain first and foremost, and stop pandering to the EU.

References:

http://www.theguardian.com/world/2013/jul/01/eu-extend-soviet-union-david-cameron

http://www.nytimes.com/2012/10/25/opinion/hillary-clinton-catherine-ashton-ukraines-election.html

10. Accusations of racism by the Lib Dems

To: Somerset Guardian

I strongly object to the Liberal Democrats accusing UKIP of racism. UKIP welcomes new members regardless of their ethnic origin.

An official Lib Dem briefing note accuses UKIP of racism, quote: 'Others will simply be repulsed by their anti-Europeanism and racism. But understanding where UKIP's voters are coming from and how we should approach it are important. It's important however not to panic. But it's also important not to believe that it's our job, alone, to respond to their lies.'

UKIP is not anti-European, it is anti-EU. The Lib Dems appear to be confused, or else they are deliberately and dishonestly misrepresenting the issue. I would like to see all European countries break free of the shackles of the EU, and to be free to trade on an equal footing with the whole world. All empires eventually crumble, the EU will too.

It is a bit rich that the Lib Dems should accuse UKIP of lying. It was Conservative Prime Minister Edward Heath who caused us to join the EU, the EEC as it was then, on the false basis that it was merely a Common Market. Now the EU is hell-bent on a path of ever greater union, currency union and of necessity political union to go with the currency union. It even has its own nascent armed forces and will be using airborne drones.

Nigel Farage has made clear the position of UKIP regarding racism:
"UKIP is a free-thinking, egalitarian party opposed to racism, sectarianism and extremism.
UKIP is dedicated to liberty, opportunity, equality under the law

and the aspirations of the British people. We will always act in the interests of Britain, especially on immigration, employment, energy supply and fisheries.

We know that only by leaving the European Union can we regain control of our borders, our parliament, our democracy and our ability to trade freely with the fastest-growing economies in the world. A referendum to allow the country to decide this matter will create the greatest opportunity for national renewal in our lifetime."

References:

http://www.express.co.uk/news/uk/463237/Ukip-fury-after-leaked-Lib-Dem-dossier-labels-supporters-racist

11. Clegg pro Britain?

To: Western Daily Press

Nick Clegg has said something during the Liberal Democrat conference that is similar to the words spoken by Nigel Farage. Are their positions in fact closer than we realise?

Nick Clegg said: "We don't like Europe for Europe's sake. I think we should be members of the European Union for Britain's sake."

Nigel Farage has said: "We will always act in the interests of Britain, especially on immigration, employment, energy supply and fisheries."

Clegg has by his own words clearly abandoned any principles of the European high ideals - to share the benefits and burdens of the union between nations. It is hardly a strong argument for the Lib Dems to be the party of 'in' the EU.

All that is now required for Farage to defeat Clegg in the forthcoming debates is to show that the EU in fact costs Britain more than it benefits Britain. The cost is in terms of uncontrolled immigration, depressed wages, youth unemployment, red tape, rising demand for housing, building on green belt, energy insecurity, and that we have to keep on bailing out the EU which repeatedly fails to balance its books and in which corruption and wastefulness are rife. These burdens are of course a problem throughout the EU. Other nations would benefit from leaving too.

References:

Asked why the conference is focusing on Europe when "nobody on the doorstep cares", Mr Clegg says: "People do care about work, about money in their pockets, they do worry about crime, they do worry about climate change, and we will not do anything about these things unless we work with other countries.

"We don't like Europe for Europe's sake. I think we should be members of the European Union for Britain's sake. If we're not part of the club, you can't stand on doorsteps saying you are fighting for jobs if the Tories and UKIP pull us out. You can't stand on doorsteps saying you're fighting to keep communities safe. You can't stand on doorsteps saying you're doing everything you can to fight flooding and other climate change events."

References:

http://www.yorkpress.co.uk/NEWS/11062325.Liberal_Democrat_confere nce_in_York__live_blog___day_2/

12. Green Party pro-EU

To: Western Daily Press

The Green Party stance on our EU membership must surely be contrary to environmental principles.

The letter by the Green Group leader of Stroud District Council Prof Molly Scott Cato (Daily Press 11 March) states: 'The Green Party is committed to staying in Europe and will be fighting the May's European elections on that platform'. I do agree with her statement that Nick Clegg is 'desperate but also dishonest'.

Our membership of the EU means that we have no control of our borders. We cannot prevent a large number of people coming to the UK from EU countries. David Cameron pledged to bring net migration down to a few tens of thousands per annum. He made that pledge before the 2010 general election and I believed him at the time. Now with net migration increasing to 212,000 it is obvious that Cameron is powerless to control our borders.

The Green Party wishes to reduce our CO_2 emissions. The CO_2 emissions of the UK is high at 8.5 tonnes per capita per annum. Other countries in the EU whose citizens are moving to the UK in significant numbers have lower emissions per capita. For example Poland 8.3, Italy 7.5, Spain 7.4, Bulgaria 6.7, France 6.1, Lithuania 4.6, Romania 4.4, Latvia 3.4 tonnes per person per annum.

The atmosphere does not care from which country the CO_2 is emitted. It makes no logical sense at all from an environmental perspective to encourage the movement of people from countries with low per capita emissions to countries such as the UK with high per capita emissions. Logically the Green Party should be campaigning for the UK to have proper control of our borders, which is not possible while we are members of the EU.

13. Bath up for grabs

To: The Independent

Steve Richards visited Bath recently and has made the observation: 'The Lib Dems face a daunting challenge at the next election. I spent a few days in Bath last week, a seat currently held by them, and kept on bumping into people who had voted for Clegg's party last time but who insist they will not do so next year even if that means the constituency elects a Tory MP.'

It is true that the popularity of the Lib Dems has plummeted nationally. They cannot rely on the incumbency factor in Bath because the Lib Dem MP Don Foster will be retiring in 2015. Labour do not have much support in Bath, however it is not at all certain that the Tory candidate would be elected. UKIP has a local candidate, Julian Deverell, who has plenty of good contacts and roots locally. The Tory candidate has been parachuted in from London, and his campaigning to date has been sporadic. UKIP has an excellent chance of electoral success in Bath.

The first King of all England, Edgar the Peaceable, was crowned in Bath in 973, in the Anglo-Saxon Abbey Church. It would be fitting for a patriotic Englishman to be elected to represent Bath in 2015.

References:

Bath UKIP candidate
http://www.bathchronicle.co.uk/UKIP-chooses-Julian-Deverell-general-election/story-20696671-detail/story.html

No pact between UKIP and Tories in Bath & North East Somerset
http://www.bathchronicle.co.uk/UKIP-votes-pact-Tories-Bath-North-East-Somerset/story-19938801-detail/story.html

14. EU membership is not green

To: Bath Chronicle

It does seem extraordinary that the Green Party is supporting our membership of the EU. (Nicholas Hales, letters 13 March)

The UK population size is already unsustainable from an environmental perspective. Net migration has increased to 212,000 because we cannot control the numbers arriving from EU countries whilst we are still a member of the EU.

The Green Party wishes to reduce our CO_2 emissions. The CO_2 emissions of the UK is high at 8.5 tonnes per capita per annum. Other countries in the EU whose citizens are moving to the UK in significant numbers have lower emissions per capita. For example Poland 8.3, Italy 7.5, Spain 7.4, Bulgaria 6.7, France 6.1, Lithuania 4.6, Romania 4.4, Latvia 3.4 tonnes per person per annum.

The atmosphere does not care from which country the CO_2 is emitted. It makes no logical sense at all from an environmental perspective to encourage the movement of people from countries with low per capita emissions to countries such as the UK with high per capita emissions. Logically the Green Party should be campaigning for the UK to have proper control of our borders, which is not possible while we are members of the EU. I hope that they will review their policy on EU membership. Common sense tells us that the current migration figures are not sustainable.

References:

http://en.wikipedia.org/wiki/List_of_countries_by_carbon_dioxide_emiss ions_per_capita

15. Labour hypocrisy on housing

To: Somerset Guardian

The Labour candidate for North East Somerset has criticised Jacob Rees-Mogg MP for his concern regarding housing developments on green belt land whilst his mother Lady Rees-Mogg applied for planning permission to build 19 houses in a village in his constituency. (Somerset Guardian 13 March.)

Labour have quite rightly highlighted this inconsistency of message. However they fail to address the root cause of our housing crisis and hence the need to build many thousands of new houses in the constituency. Under the Labour government immigration and consequently the demand for housing skyrocketed, as a deliberate ploy to gain the votes of immigrants for their party. This is at the expense of the living standards of their traditional voters, in terms of jobs, downward pressure on wages and upward pressure on rents. Many ex-Labour voters feel betrayed and are turning to UKIP.

Net migration has increased to 212,000 per annum despite the pledge of David Cameron to bring it down to a few tens of thousands. He cannot control arrivals from the EU whilst we are still in the EU. Around 80% of those polled are worried about excessive migration, and yet Labour will not give us a referendum on our EU membership. Leaving the EU is our only realistic way to regain control of our borders, EU officials have already made it clear to Cameron that he is not permitted to stop the thousands of arrivals from Europe. We have lost our sovereignty over our own borders.

References:

http://www.somersetguardian.co.uk/Lady-Rees-Mogg-8217-s-planning-application-19/story-20805743-detail/story.html

16. Tribute to Bob Crow and Tony Benn

To: Western Daily Press

The left wing of the political spectrum has lost two genuine conviction men of character - Bob Crow and Tony Benn. They were men of steel, we seem to have plastic imitation 'professional' politicians now who sound far from convincing or trustworthy.

Both these men were strongly anti-European Union. For Bob Crow it was because of the undermining of wages due to an excessive supply of cheap workers. For Tony Benn it was the loss of our sovereignty, and loss of democratic principles which are at stake.

Tony Benn stated in Parliament: "For many years it has rightly been a principle of this House that no Parliament can bind its successors. In European Union every decision binds its successors because one cannot change it. Even if a British Government were elected on the issue of repealing a piece of this legislation, prospective Members of Parliament would not be able to tell the electorate that they would repeal it because the mechanism to do so would not exist. European Community legislation is like a lobster pot - it is easy to get in but very difficult to get out."

Unfortunately the Labour leader Ed Miliband does not appear to understand what is at stake, and is reluctant to give the electorate a referendum on our EU membership. The EU is dragging us down and compounding our problems.

References:

http://tony-benn.blogspot.co.uk/

17. Rees-Mogg cloning

To: Somerset Guardian

The MP for North East Somerset Jacob Rees-Mogg has spoken on the topic of mitochondrial donation. Every cell of our body contains mitochondria which we inherit along the maternal line. If they are faulty then that fault can have a serious effect on our health because the mitochondria are the 'power stations' of the cell. The technique replaces the faulty mitochondria with good ones. Modern medical science offers us some truly remarkable opportunities to alleviate human suffering.

Mr Rees-Mogg has fundamentally misunderstood the technique, describing it as cloning and as genetic modification. Neither of his statements are correct. It does not have an exact equivalent, but we should think of it more in terms of grafting a shoot of a fruit tree onto a root stock, or of organ donation.

In order to successfully navigate the modern world it is vitally important that our elected representatives have a good grasp of the topics on which they make pronouncements. Otherwise they are at risk of simply wasting the valuable debating time in Parliament. Our country faces many challenges in the 21st century, we urgently need Members of Parliament who are equally familiar with the events and opportunities of this century as they are familiar with the events of previous centuries.

References:

http://www.bionews.org.uk/page_405551.asp

http://www.publications.parliament.uk/pa/cm201314/cmhansrd/cm140312/halltext/140312h0002.htm

18. Liam Fox on EU elites

To: Western Daily Press

Dr Liam Fox the MP for North Somerset is absolutely correct when he criticises the European Union:

"The heavily cosseted and pampered European political class in Brussels are only too willing to blame the citizens of the EU for the rise of political extremes on both left and right of the spectrum. They seem congenitally incapable of asking themselves whether it is their behaviour and their political brittleness that is the primary driver of this process."

Fortunately in Britain we have UKIP, a party opposed to extremism and racism. In Greece the far right has become prominent. Democratic principles in the very nation where democracy was invented have been usurped by the EU. What arrogance!

Dr Fox has a boss who acts on behalf of the expansionist EU machine. It should instead be the duty of David Cameron to always act in the best interests of Britain. Unfortunately this is not the case. During his visit to Kazakhstan in the summer of 2013 he said:

"Britain has always supported the widening of the EU. Our vision of the EU is that it should be a large trading and co-operating organisation that effectively stretches, as it were, from the Atlantic to the Urals."

Clearly Cameron wants Ukraine to join the EU. The Urals are some 800 miles east of Ukraine, an area which includes Moscow. Where did this policy originate? I do not recall the inclusion of Moscow into the EU being the vision of Britain. Is Cameron provoking Russia on his own or is he under instructions from the EU? The consequences are inevitable.

Dr Fox should act according to his conscience and join UKIP.

References:

http://www.express.co.uk/news/uk/465349/European-elite-s-refusal-to-accept-change-is-fuelling-extremism-warns-leading-Tory

http://www.theguardian.com/world/2013/jul/01/eu-extend-sovietunion-david-cameron

http://www.nytimes.com/2012/10/25/opinion/hillary-clinton-catherineashton-ukraines-election.html

19. The view from Stonehenge

To: Western Daily Press

North Wiltshire MP James Gray is correct to be concerned
regarding the location of the proposed barracks in line with the
summer solstice sunrise at Stonehenge. It would indeed be
helpful if they could be located away from the prominent axis of
the 4,500 year old monument.

Stonehenge is even more remarkable than most people realise. As
with the shape of the wing of Concorde, form follows function to
more or less automatically evolve an aesthetically pleasing
structure. Stonehenge has a unique form and so it is fascinating to
consider its function. If you will visit the Youtube website and
search for 'Stonehenge Astronomical Observatory', you will be
introduced to my own theory regarding its function. It is even
more advanced than I had anticipated when first stepping out on
the journey of discovery. The mathematical concept which
underpins the implementation was a world first as far as I can tell,
pre-dating the same concept ascribed to the Babylonian
astronomers by well over a thousand years.

We must be careful to preserve that which is good and
worthwhile in Britain, whether it is ancient monuments or our
values, our own laws, our customs, our sense of fair play, our
tolerance and good humour, our own sovereignty and our own
governance. We are exceedingly fortunate to have inherited this
legacy, it is our duty to maintain this legacy and pass it to future
generations unharmed. Mr Gray is correct to express his concern.

How would the inspired creators of Stonehenge view us today? It
turns out that we are not so distant from them, they gave us an
understanding of geometry upon which so much technological
progress is based.

20. EU elections

To: Bath Chronicle

It is a shame that the Liberal Democrat contributors to this letters page have not included any apology for the racism accusation made against UKIP. I highlighted that an official Lib Dem briefing note has made that accusation.

Never mind, they can avoid doing the right thing if they wish, the electorate will notice. UKIP is in first place in the recent ComRes opinion poll at 30% whilst the Lib Dems languish at 8% for the forthcoming European elections.

On average the threshold for gaining an MEP seat is 12%, it is entirely possible that the Lib Dems will have zero MEPs elected on the 22 May. Sir Graham Watson can then stop worrying about prunes and the inadequacies of the European Food Safety Authority!

It is important to register to vote if you are not yet on the Electoral Roll. You can do so via the Electoral Commission website, the Bath & North East Somerset Council website, or by phoning them or email on 01225 477333 elections@bathnes.gov.uk

Please do use your vote. Important principles are at stake. I would vote in a referendum for our sovereignty and our democracy to be restored, if the Liberal 'Democrats' would permit me to do so.

References:
http://www.express.co.uk/news/uk/463237/Ukip-fury-after-leaked-Lib-Dem-dossier-labels-supporters-racist
http://www.bathnes.gov.uk/services/your-council-and-democracy/elections/voting-post
http://www.bathchronicle.co.uk/UKIP-racist/story-20802974-detail/story.html

21. The Alan Turing Institute

To: Western Daily Press

Alan Turing, the mathematical genius, is to be remembered. His role role as a codebreaker during WW II contributed to saving thousands of lives and shortened the war. The Alan Turing Institute is to be set up in his honour. (Daily Press 22 March)

The tragedy of his life is that, despite all that he achieved for our democratic freedoms and for saving us from Nazi oppression, he was persecuted due to his homosexuality. He died at the age of forty-one due to cyanide poisoning, a suspected suicide.

During my years working in the defence industry I have been privileged to work alongside similar highly intelligent colleagues who happened to be homosexual. Sexual orientation is no barrier to patriotism. Our freedoms are hard won and if we are not careful, are easily lost.

References:

http://www.westerndailypress.co.uk/Code-breaker-honoured-institute/story-20841869-detail/story.html?ito=email_newsletter_westerndailypress

22. The housing crisis and the Liberal Democrats

To: Western Daily Press

The Liberal Democrats simply do not 'get it', do they? Or they are being blatantly dishonest and hoping that the electorate do not notice.

Lib Dem MP David Heath has complained in Parliament about all the extra housing which is being built on green belt, and spoiling villages in his Somerton and Frome constituency. (Daily Press 24th March) There is a direct causal link between our membership of the European Union, a large and increasing net migration figure, and the need to build hundreds of thousands of extra houses. When your village or town is spoiled, and you are stuck in a traffic jam due to the inadequate road capacity for all the extra cars, you know that it is the Lib Dems who are to blame with their fanatical and unquestioning support for the EU.

I am very much looking forward to the debates between Nigel Farage and Nick Clegg. The first is on Wednesday 26th March at 7 pm on LBC Radio. The second is on BBC2 on Wednesday 2nd April. My vote is for good old fashioned common sense.

If the Liberal Democrats are unable to see the direct linkage between our EU membership and the demand for all the extra houses then they are not fit to be in office. If they can see it, but are too dishonest to admit that this is the case, then they are also not fit to be in office!

References:

http://www.westerndailypress.co.uk/Countryside-siege-developers-planning-appeals/story-20844466-detail/story.html

23. Horse meat

To: Western Daily Press

Chris Rundle is absolutely correct to highlight the problems relating to food quality and traceability. ('Let's not swallow the lie that the horsemeat scandal has trotted off' Daily Press 26 March). He pointed out that that the number of tests to verify the composition of food had about halved over five years.

We do need to be aware that the Food Standards Agency has overall responsibility in the UK for ensuring our food quality. They are however working to instructions set by the European Food Safety Authority! The website of the FSA states: 'Much of the detailed legislation on food standards originates in the European Union. This section includes details on how food hygiene legislation was consolidated and simplified as well as details of other European legislation.'

The website of the European Food Safety Authority states: 'EFSA's independent scientific advice underpins the European food safety system. Thanks to this system, European consumers are among the best protected and best informed in the world as regards risks in the food chain.'

Sir Graham Watson the Lib Dem MEP for the south west region has already highlighted the inadequacies of the European Food Safety Authority. The horse meat scandal and the problems that Chris Rundle has highlighted are telling us that we have to reclaim control of our own food, and not rely on the EU authorities to ensure the quality of it.

References:
http://www.westerndailypress.co.uk/Chris-Rundle-Let-s-swallow-lie-horsemeat-scandal/story-20851376-detail/story.html
http://www.food.gov.uk/enforcement/regulation/
http://www.efsa.europa.eu/en/aboutefsa.htm

24. Farage Clegg debate

To: Western Daily Press

What a cracking debate we had between Nigel Farage and Nick Clegg on LBC and Sky.
We have round two to look forward to on BBC2 on 2 April.

Clegg trotted off his usual asinine arguments in favour of our European Union membership, that we would lose three million jobs if we left, and that it would be difficult for police forces to catch international criminals. Both these arguments were easily demolished by Farage, who pointed out that the author of the original academic study regarding jobs had already stated that the Lib Dems were misrepresenting the results of his work. The argument regarding international criminals is also nonsense. UK police have worked with INTERPOL for many years, and this organisation is truly international with one hundred and ninety member countries, not limited to the EU countries. The UK joined the predecessor organisation, the International Criminal Police Commission in 1928.

Clegg is not being logical, Farage ran rings around him with good common sense responses. The worrying thing is that the Lib Dems appear to believe their own mistaken ideas, despite the evidence to the contrary being pointed out to them.

The fact that Clegg even challenged Farage to a debate demonstrates that the Lib Dems are absolutely desperate. Their poll rating for the European elections on 22 May show that they may have zero MEPs or at best two or three. If their current poll rating continues until the general election next year they may then have just eleven MPs.

Meanwhile Nigel Farage and UKIP are on a roll. A recent ComRes poll for the European elections puts UKIP in first place, narrowly ahead of Labour and well ahead of the Conservatives. The debates can only boost UKIP even more!

25. Response to letter from the Green Party

To: Bath Chronicle

I thank Nicholas Hales of the Green Party for his reply to my letter. We do need a serious debate regarding our membership of the EU, on a range of issues. Of particular concern, I assume, for the Green Party, is the effect of our EU membership on the UK emissions of carbon dioxide.

My point, focusing on the narrow issue of carbon dioxide emissions is: why would the Green Party support the movement of people from countries with low emissions per capita to countries such as the UK with high emissions per capita? For example Romania and Latvia have approximately half the emissions per capita of the UK.

The consequence of the movement of people to the UK from countries with low per capita emissions is that overall emissions will go up. Is this what the Green Party wants? It is a consequence of our membership of the European Union. Knowing this, why does the Green Party support our EU membership? Do they think it is beneficial that the UK population has increased rapidly? Our population size is already unsustainable, we are a net importer of food for example. Can they please reconsider their EU membership policy? We need to be logical, for the sake of future generations.

References:

http://www.bathchronicle.co.uk/Immigration-facts/story-20856776-detail/story.html

http://en.wikipedia.org/wiki/List_of_countries_by_carbon_dioxide_emissions_per_capita

26. EU culpability in Ukraine

To: Western Daily Press

During the debate between Nigel Farage and Nick Clegg on LBC, Mr Farage stated that the EU has blood on its hands regarding Ukraine. He is correct, here is the smoking gun: In October 2012 in a joint communication by Hillary Clinton and Baroness Ashton they stated: 'The European Union and Ukraine have completed negotiations on an ambitious Association Agreement that will provide for the country's political association and economic integration with the European Union..' Baroness Ashton is the High Representative of the European Union for foreign affairs and security policy.

In July 2013 David Cameron visited Kazakhstan and said: "Britain has always supported the widening of the EU. Our vision of the EU is that it should be a large trading and co-operating organisation that effectively stretches, as it were, from the Atlantic to the Urals." This of course means that Cameron wants Ukraine to join the EU. The Urals are well inside Russia, does Cameron want Moscow to be in the EU too? His vision is absurd.

The expansionist EU has clearly angered the Russian government. It cannot be any surprise that there has been a reaction. Far from keeping the peace in Europe, for which the EU received a Nobel prize in 2012, the actions of Baroness Ashton and David Cameron have been deeply destabilising. The world needs buffer states such as Turkey, Ukraine, and at one time Tibet, they provide a key role in maintaining stability. It would be ironic if Putin were to receive the next Nobel peace prize.

References:

http://www.theguardian.com/world/2013/jul/01/eu-extend-soviet-union-david-cameron

http://www.nytimes.com/2012/10/25/opinion/hillary-clinton-catherine-ashton-ukraines-election.html

27. Calamity Cable

To: Western Daily Press

The economics guru of the Liberal Democrats has caused a significant financial loss to the taxpayer. Will Vince Cable have the common decency to apologise for undervaluing Royal Mail? We have lost £2.3 billion due to him undervaluing the share price, according to the National Audit Office.

What is the point of all the austerity pain, if the Lib Dems simply throw away our money like confetti? Still, they are wedded to the idea that the EU is good for us! It is no wonder that the electorate are disenchanted with them. For them the honeymoon period will be well and truly over on the 22nd May.

References:

http://www.dailymail.co.uk/news/article-2593790/Taxpayers-lost-2-3bn-cheap-Royal-Mail-sell-Government-watchdogs-report-lays-bare-city-hit-jackpot-sale.html

28. Riddle

To: Western Daily Press

Those who wish to be out will be in, and those who wish to be in will be out! This sounds like a Zen riddle, it is instead the choice we can make on the 22nd May. UKIP is ahead in the polls while the Lib Dems are struggling to retain any MEPs.

It is vitally important for your own future and for the sake of future generations that you cast your vote - register via your local authority or via the Electoral Commission website.

I feel that we should be outward looking to benefit from the opportunities that the whole world offers, not inward looking to the EU trading bloc. We are a seafaring nation, it does not suit our national character to be hidebound by pettyfogging laws emanating from Brussels. No wonder our MPs are idle in Parliament, three quarters of our laws originate from the twenty eight commissioners of the EU. In the European election your vote is worth one tenth of that of a voter in Luxembourg or Malta! This is not democratic. Why do the Liberal 'Democrats' support this lack of equality of votes? They also opposed fairer constituency sizes in the UK.

Only around a third of us bother to vote in the European elections and yet over half of us want to get out of the EU. If you wish to have democracy then vote for the party which believes in democracy!

References:
http://www.jhubc.it/ecpr-porto/virtualpaperroom/125.pdf
http://www.euractiv.com/uk-europe/52-brits-vote-leave-eu-tomorrow-news-532867
http://www.ceps.eu/files/book/1886.pdf
http://blogs.independent.co.uk/2014/03/15/ukip-leading-in-euro-elections-race/

29. Grudge match

To: Western Daily Press

In a bitterly contested match Farage vs Clegg, 'out' vs 'in', the result is a resounding score of 7 goals to 3 in favour of Farage.

Clegg behaved badly, repeatedly attacking the player rather than the ball in a sign of desperation and contempt for the rules of the game. It was more or less a foregone conclusion that he would lose, the question remains: why on earth did Clegg ever think that it was a good idea to challenge Farage at all? It demonstrates that Clegg has a dangerously out of touch arrogance. Blinded by his own propaganda he simply could not perceive how weak his arguments really are. His childish naïveté that roaming charges for mobile phones was a good reason for being in the EU is laughable. The phone companies will recoup the cost by increasing other charges.

Even when in the closing minutes Clegg was presented with an open goal: "what will the EU be like in ten years?" he tapped the ball with no energy at all, and it rolled wide of the net. We can see that he had already lost belief in the core principles of the EU from his comment at the Lib Dem spring conference: "We don't like Europe for Europe's sake". His team faces relegation in the forthcoming European elections. It is probable that the manager will be sacked, and that would be well deserved indeed.

References:
http://www.theguardian.com/politics/blog/2014/apr/02/farage-v-clegg-the-debate-for-europe-politics-live-blog

http://www.telegraph.co.uk/news/newstopics/eureferendum/10740795/Nigel-Farage-scores-victory-over-Nick-Clegg-as-second-TV-debate-turns-nasty.html

http://www.yorkpress.co.uk/NEWS/11062325.Liberal_Democrat_conference_in_York%20%20_live_blog___day_2/

30. What is the Labour party policy on the EU?

To: Western Daily Press

Given that Nick Clegg has so dismally failed to put the case for our continued EU membership, and that opinion polls show that the Lib Dems may end up with no MEPs at all in a few weeks time, my question is: what is the policy of the Labour Party regarding the EU? Are they in or are they out? Do they want to be tarred with the Lib Dem brush, or will they acknowledge the many failings of the EU? I have examined the Labour website. It tells me about Ed Miliband, Harriet Harman, their shadow cabinet, their MPs and their parliamentary candidates for Westminster. How strange that their website does not seem to even mention the European elections on the 22 May!

Perhaps this is a deliberate ploy, they do not wish to be associated with the EU, which is causing so much harm to the electoral prospects of the Lib Dems, and is tearing the Conservative party in two. If Labour really do not care about the European election then they should say so, and have the common decency to stand down their MEP candidates. At the moment the silence is deafening. If we cannot know what their EU policy is, then they do not deserve even a single vote.

References:

http://www.labour.org.uk/home

31. What is the Labour party policy on the EU? (Telegraph)

To: The Daily Telegraph

Given that Nick Clegg has so dismally failed to put the case for our continued EU membership, and that opinion polls show that the Lib Dems may end up with no MEPs at all in a few weeks time, my question is: what is the policy of the Labour Party regarding the EU? Are they in or are they out? Do they want to be tarred with the Lib Dem brush, or will they acknowledge the need for EU reform? I have examined the Labour website. It tells me about Ed Miliband, Harriet Harman, their shadow cabinet, their MPs and their parliamentary candidates. How strange that their website does not seem to even mention the European elections on 22 May! If the electorate cannot know what their EU policy is, then Labour do not deserve even a single vote.

References:

http://www.labour.org.uk/home

32. Vince Cable MP on housing

To: Western Daily Press

Vince Cable MP, the Lib Dem business guru has woken up to the fact that housing is becoming even more unaffordable. He has correctly pointed out that even those on good salaries are struggling to get a foot onto the housing ladder.

Too many adult sons and daughters are still living with their parents because of the high cost of rents and mortgages. They are unable to live a conventional adult life, get married and start a family. For far too many people their life is on hold. Why is this?

During the 1970s when the UK population was shrinking, the number of homes built was around 400, 000 per year. From the late 1990s the population has increased at a steep rate and yet there are now around 200, 000 homes built per year. It does not take a business guru to understand that house prices would increase rapidly too. Unfortunately we have no control at all over the UK population increase because of the EU laws on free movement. The inevitable consequence is that millions of extra houses will need to be built, many on green belt land. Alternatively we simply have to exit the EU which we joined in 1972. We have to question the benefits of our EU membership, the costs are all too painfully apparent.

References:

http://www.independent.co.uk/news/uk/politics/exclusive-housing-bubble-brewing-as-prices-become-unaffordable-for-middle-earners-says-business-secretary-vince-cable-9236587.html

http://www.insidehousing.co.uk/development/the-new-players/6506880.article

33. Response to letter from Nick Hales regarding diesel pollution

To: Bath Chronicle

I read with interest the letter by Nick Hales of the Green Party regarding his suggestion for a bridge across the Avon linking the A36 with the A363. His suggestion raises more questions than it answers. He is concerned about the pollution from lorries coming in to Bath. Diesel engines do indeed produce more particulates than petrol engines, although they are more efficient than petrol engines and hence produce less carbon dioxide per mile. Carbon dioxide (CO_2) is the gas which we naturally breathe out and plants breathe in. Diesel and smoke particulates lodge in our lungs and can cause health problems.

In order to make an informed decision regarding a bridge, we firstly need to understand what proportion of lorries are just passing through Bath, and what proportion are making deliveries. If most of them are making deliveries then it is not practical to stop them. Also what proportion of coaches are travelling in to the centre of Bath for tourists to visit our wonderful city? Mr Hales suggests that they would also be diverted. He studiously fails to mention that buses also have diesel engines, I would be interested to know what he proposes for buses in Bath.

My additional question for Mr Hales: do you think that it is preferable to use wood burning stoves or gas boilers? The former produce low net carbon dioxide but high particulates, the latter do produce carbon dioxide and low particulates. If everybody in Bath were to operate a wood burning stove I imagine that the airborne particulate count would be far higher than it currently is. What is the Green Party policy on particulates from wood burning stoves in cities?

34. Nigel Farage and Stop UKIP visiting Bath

To: Bath Chronicle

With UKIP making headlines recently for the right reasons, and topping the polls for the European election which takes place on 22 May, we also have a double treat for Bath residents to enjoy.

The Stop UKIP comedy act will be performing at the Rondo Theatre on 24 April. From the preview video of their act I can see that it may appeal to some who want their prejudiced views to be reinforced. However, for those wanting a true perspective of the party, on 29 April the leader of UKIP Nigel Farage will be speaking at a public meeting at the Forum in central Bath. Tickets are free but need to be booked. The details are on the events page of the Bath UKIP website.

It is highly unlikely that UKIP will be stopped by a pair of comedians. After all, Nick Clegg has failed to do so, and David Cameron has also failed. In my opinion UKIP is becoming more like a movement for the restoration of our freedoms, our democracy and our sovereignty than merely a political party. An increasing number of the electorate understand what UKIP is about, and they like what they see. We know that the establishment is seriously worried, because of the level of vilification that the party has been receiving. Why not go along to both events and make up your own mind?

References:

http://www.rondotheatre.co.uk/production/1068/

http://www.bathukip.org.uk/events/?event_id1=126

35. Taxpayer funded Lib Dem strategist

To: Western Daily Press

The Liberal Democrats have serious questions to answer regarding the salary of their head of strategy Ryan Coetzee. His generous salary of £110,000 is alleged to be paid for by the taxpayer. It should of course be paid for by their own party, backdated to when he started in 2012.

The Lib Dems have slumped in the opinion polls down to a new low of 6% following the debates between Nigel Farage and Nick Clegg. This is hardly surprising as the debates highlighted just how far divorced from reality Clegg really is. For example he insisted that 'only' 7% of our laws originated in Brussels. And yet the EU Commissioner for Justice Viviane Reding has publicly stated that around 75% to 80% of our national laws now originate from EU Directives. Who do you think you are kidding Mr Clegg, if you think we are so dumb?

Maybe it was Mr Coetzee who suggested that the debates would boost the Lib Dems? Instead it has destroyed them and it would not be surprising if they have zero MEPs elected on 22 May. If indeed he is responsible for the destruction of the Lib Dems then his generous salary is worth every penny as he has done us all a favour!

References:
http://www.dailymail.co.uk/news/article-2604782/Nick-Clegg-questions-answer-revealed-pays-election-gurur-Ryan-Coetzee-110-000-taxpayer-cash.html

http://www.libdemvoice.org/latest-icm-poll-lib-dems-at-12-for-westminster-but-just-6-in-the-euros-39359.html

https://www.youtube.com/watch?v=Qb-6fZa8Vok

36. What is the Labour Party policy on the EU?

To: Somerset Guardian

With only a few weeks to go before the European election on 22 May, we must think about our own feelings about the EU. UKIP will probably come first in this election, but what about the party in second place? What is the Labour Party policy on our EU membership? Are they in favour of it like the Lib Dems or against it like UKIP? Looking at the Labour website, there is nothing about this election. Are they desperately trying to ignore the issues? Why should they expect anybody to vote for them if they do not make their position clear?

There is a significant divide within Labour about the EU. One of the main donors to Labour is Len McCluskey the leader of the Unite union. He is ready to form a breakaway political party, a left wing anti-EU party, with the support of fifteen Labour MPs and £6 million of union money. Bob Crow the recently deceased leader of the RMT union was staunchly anti-EU, because he could clearly see how wages are pushed down by cheap eastern European workers.

If you think that you are supportive of the EU, please look carefully at what it is doing. EU Commissioner Viviane Reding has stated that 75% to 80% of our national laws originate from EU Directives. The EU is forming its own armed cross border police force, the EU will have its own military equipment including drones. It has meddled in Ukraine with the disastrous consequences that we now see, following David Cameron stating that he wants the EU to extend to the Ural mountains! The Urals are deep inside Russia! Cameron has lost the plot, Ed Miliband is dithering, and Nick Clegg has lost the argument. It is my belief that only UKIP are acting in the best interests of Britain.

References:

https://www.youtube.com/watch?v=Qb-6fZa8Vok

http://www.theguardian.com/world/2013/jul/01/eu-extend-soviet-union-davidcameron

http://www.nytimes.com/2012/10/25/opinion/hillary-clinton-catherine-ashtonukraines-election.html

http://www.independent.co.uk/news/uk/politics/unite-union-boss-len-mccluskey-threatens-to-launch-party-to-rival-labour-9231266.html

http://www.thesun.co.uk/sol/homepage/news/politics/5566801/Red-Lenin-steals-Labour-MPs-for-new-lefties-party.html

http://www.powerinaunion.co.uk/excellent-interview-with-unites-len-mccluskey/

37. UKIP common sense for B&NES

To: Bath Chronicle

The Liberal Democrats are making themselves deeply unpopular in Bath. The bus gate in Dorchester Street has collected a whopping £270,000 of fines in just a month. I know a number of people who have been caught out, and they will certainly never again vote for the Lib Dems! The Lib Dems are prominent on B&NES Council, and seem to be impervious to common sense.

I am standing as the UKIP candidate for the Bathavon North ward, which includes Bathampton, Batheaston, Bathford, and Claverton, and extends across the rural area north of Bath. The by election is on the same day as the European election, 22 May. Anybody not yet registered to vote needs to get onto the electoral roll straight away. I have met people who have not voted for many years, and yet they are voting for UKIP this time. I see UKIP as more of a movement than just a political party.

If elected to B&NES Council I will do all I can to ensure that good old fashioned common sense prevails. I would certainly oppose misguided projects such as the bus gate in Dorchester Street. The UKIP Local Manifesto 2014 states: 'We refuse to be politically driven or politically correct and will always stand up for local people and common sense, rather than toeing the party line. This is often a shock for politicians from the old parties, but is the shot in the arm that our town halls need.' The Manifesto can be downloaded from the UKIP website www.ukip.org, please read it and make your voting decision based upon it.

References:

http://www.bathchronicle.co.uk/New-signs-controversial-Dorchester-Street-bus/story-21013561-detail/story.html

http://www.ukip.org/

38. Green Party public meeting

To: Bath Chronicle

To: Dursley Gazette

To: Stroud News & Journal, Stroud Life

Several members of UKIP attended the Green Party public meeting in Bath on St George's Day. The panellists spoke well, it was a pity that they had only a small audience as there were important matters discussed. Molly Scott-Cato, their MEP candidate opened her speech by describing how we must preserve the beauty of our green and pleasant land. I fully agree with this point, and was moved by her depth of feeling. She was proud that she had played a role in preventing a housing development near Stroud which would have spoiled the Slad Valley.

I asked a question relating to solar farms: With solar farms springing up and covering many hundreds of acres of farmland with aesthetically ugly black panels, does Molly think that if we are to have solar panels, it would be better to put them on roofs rather than on farmland? She agreed with me! My further point is that it takes the land out of production, often grade 3 land, which could be used for growing crops such as potatoes or for grazing. It implies that we would need to import more food, adding to food miles and hence CO_2 emissions. The solar farms may not be as eco-friendly as their proponents would claim.

I do not understand why the Green Party is pro-EU, since we therefore have no control of our borders and hence cannot limit the growth of the UK population. It is already unsustainable. Nevertheless I do respect the Green Party, they are driven by principles rather than opportunism. I am delighted to see that a recent opinion poll puts them ahead of the Lib Dems for the European election. The Lib Dems have cynically been considering forming a coalition with Labour next time. Nick Clegg has been a disaster, with a poor sense of judgement.

39. Labour EU votes

To: Western Daily Press

A recent opinion poll for Sky News puts Labour well behind UKIP for the European election. UKIP are on 31 percent and Labour is in second place with 25 percent.

I am having difficulty discovering what the Labour Party policy is on the European Union. On their website there is plenty of information about Ed Miliband, Harriet Harman, the Shadow Cabinet, and Labour MPs. There is simply nothing about the forthcoming European election regarding their EU policy. I did find a list of the names of their MEP candidates, but no information about the candidates. It is as though they are deliberately ignoring the election, which is very strange.

If you are a lifelong Labour voter, please understand that the Labour Party is holding you in contempt. They want your vote but they will not tell you why they want it. What are they hoping to achieve by ignoring the European election? Their shrinking Nick Clegg broadcast was amusing, however it was relevant for a General Election, not for the European election or for the local elections. Labour is losing votes to UKIP, not surprisingly.

References:

http://www.labour.org.uk/candidates

http://news.sky.com/story/1259558/ukip-set-for-comfortable-win-in-euro-elections

40. Wither the Lib Dems?

To: Western Daily Press

Where are the Lib Dems going, and what do they hope to achieve?
Nick Clegg has styled his party as being 'in' the EU, which is
contrary to the prevailing public mood. He was decisively
defeated in the debates with Nigel Farage. The Lib Dems have
declined in their opinion poll ratings to the extent that they may
have no MEPs elected on the 22nd May, or one or two if they are
lucky. This is a disaster for their party, and for Nick Clegg as
leader who is responsible for it. If he has any common decency he
would resign if the election is as bad for them as predicted.

Messages by their members on the Lib Dem Voice website often
criticise Nick Clegg. The unhappiness in the ranks is plain to see.
The coalition has significantly harmed their party, as have the
broken promises and the obvious opportunism. Clegg in 2008
was calling for a referendum on our EU membership. As soon as
the Lib Dems were in government he was opposed to it, and now
that they are doing disastrously in the opinion polls he is saying
that he would no longer block it if he formed a coalition with the
Conservatives in 2015.

This man simply cannot be trusted, no doubt he will be given a
cushy job in the EU when he is dumped from British politics. He
claims to have set fire to a cactus. I do not believe him. A cactus
holds water, the Lib Dem arguments do not!

References:

http://www.newstatesman.com/politics/2014/05/why-clegg-would-
accept-eu-referendum-another-coalition

It's time for a REAL REFERENDUM ON EUROPE

It's been over THIRTY YEARS since the British people last had a vote on Britain's membership of the European Union.

That's why the Liberal Democrats want a real referendum on Europe. Only a real referendum on Britain's membership of the EU will let the people decide our country's future.

But Labour don't want the people to have their say.

The Conservatives only support a limited referendum on the Lisbon Treaty. Why won't they give the people a say in a real referendum?

Not everything is perfect with Europe, but we believe our membership has been good for our country.

In Europe we can get real action to tackle climate change. We can work together to tackle the threat of terrorism and crime. We can deliver a stronger economy for Britain.

That's why the Liberal Democrats will campaign to stay in Europe in the referendum.

But whether you agree with Europe or not, it is vital that you and the British people have a say in a real EU referendum.

Lib Dem Leader Nick Clegg: "It's time to give the British people a real referendum on Britain's membership of the European Union."

Sign our petition today

We, the undersigned, believe the Government should give the British people a real choice on Europe by holding a referendum on Britain's membership of the European Union. **www.ourcampaign.org.uk/europe**

Name_____ Tel_____

Address_____

Email_____ Mobile_____

Return to : Real Referendum Petition, 4 Cowley Street, London, SW1P 3NB

LIBERAL DEMOCRATS

41. Reply to Molly Scott Cato

To: Western Daily Press

I read with interest the letter by Molly Scott Cato of the Green Party (Daily Press 16 May). She stated 'While Ukip is a party whose morals and methods I utterly deplore, its reputed vote share of 30 per cent plus suggests that those who are finding the party's message attractive are no longer the minority of bigots and mysanthropes'.

Firstly, I would not have joined a party of bigots. UKIP is very clear that we want controlled immigration, so that we allow in to the UK only those who can make a positive contribution irrespective of their ethnic background, and not criminals and freeloaders. Secondly, if we are to regain control of our borders, the prerequisite is that we leave the EU. We have a net migration figure (immigration minus emigration) of 212,000 per annum, an increase on the previous year, and well above the 'few tens of thousands' that David Cameron pledged before he became Prime Minister. He has failed to control the numbers arriving from EU countries because he cannot do so. He was either ignorant or being dishonest when he made this pledge. Most people want a strict control of immigration.

The Green Party supports our EU membership. I find their support to be inexplicable, because the UK population growth is unsustainable form an environmental perspective. Where will all the new houses be built? Many of them on green field sites no doubt. This will be taking agricultural land out of production and we will have to import even more food, adding to food miles and hence CO_2 emissions. Rather than name calling, could the Green Party please look again at their policy regarding our EU membership, and make the inevitable common sense conclusion?

42. UKIP meeting Jacob Rees-Mogg

To: Somerset Guardian

On the Saturday before the European election and the local by-election UKIP created a presence on Batheaston High Street. We were showing our pop-up banners, leaflets, and the local election manifesto document. Several people asked for the membership form and are keen to join the party. The number of UKIP members is 37,000 and growing very rapidly, we will soon overtake the Lib Dems, whose membership figures are stagnating. Our B&NES branch membership is also growing rapidly.

The Conservatives were also active in Batheaston, making last minute deliveries of their literature. Even Jacob Rees-Mogg MP was there, they are evidently keen to win the Bathavon North by-election!

I had an informative and good-natured conversation with Jacob, reminding him of our long-standing invitation to him to join UKIP. He is a staunch EU-sceptic, and I do feel that his rightful home is in UKIP not in the Conservatives. He does have a strong loyalty to the Conservative Party, which must surely be at odds with his EU-scepticism. David Cameron and Boris Johnson both want Turkey to join the EU, Jacob responded to this point by stating that he wants us to have a strong trading relationship with Turkey. That is what I want too! We do not have to be in the EU political union in order to trade with every nation in the world. David Cameron has also called for the EU to extend far inside Russia, to the Ural mountains. We see the consequences of this provocation in the avoidable conflict in Ukraine.

If Mr Rees-Mogg wishes to be assured of retaining a seat in Parliament he has two choices: either join UKIP, or else find a safe Conservative seat elsewhere. We intend to contest the North East Somerset election with vigour. We will use many of his anti-EU arguments, and he will be obliged to agree with us!

43. UKIP election results – Bathavon North and European

To: Bath Chronicle

What a resounding result for UKIP in the European elections! There is a real feeling that we have had enough of Brussels. We cannot control our borders while we are in the EU, and hence we have no control over the number of houses which will have to be built, or the overcrowding of schools and hospitals, and pressure on roads and infrastructure.

I was delighted to stand as the UKIP candidate for Bathavon North. Although the 11 percent of the vote result was less than hoped for, in context it was not too shabby. With fewer than 40 additional votes we would have achieved third position. Labour, Lib Dems and Conservatives had been active in the ward for a long time, and had identified their supporters. We were approaching it from a standing start. In addition our branch members were spread out across the whole of B&NES delivering many thousands of the European election leaflets. We had also delivered thousands of leaflets for the visit to Bath of Nigel Farage. In the end, we did not have time to do much canvassing in the ward, in addition to two rounds of leaflets there. Next time, we will be more focussed!

The highlight of the campaign for me was the enthusiastic response that I received. People who I had never met before were shaking my hand and saying how pleased they were that I was standing. This included several people of ethnic minority origin. We in UKIP are delighted to receive their support, and for them to join our party too. I did give out membership forms during my canvassing, and these are also available from our B&NES UKIP website. For many people this will have been their first time ever to vote for UKIP, and will not be their last. We are building up momentum in B&NES, the established parties should watch out!

44. BBC Trust – Don Foster

To: Bath Chronicle

The Liberal Democrats have narrowly averted full civil war, following the disastrous results for them in the European election. Nick Clegg has been recognised as the chief cause of their difficulties, because of his courageous attempt to challenge Nigel Farage. The plot to remove Nick Clegg as their party leader has failed, there does not appear to be a credible alternative at present. Nevertheless, judging by the messages from their members on the Lib Dem Voice website, there is deep unhappiness and despair with the current structure.

I read with interest the suggestion that Don Foster MP could be considered for the role of BBC Trust chairman. There is no doubt that he could do the job. Would he want to do so? It would certainly mean stepping down from his role as whip. With so little legislation passing through Parliament, he may feel that there is not much to do anyway. Would he bring forward his retirement from Parliament, and thereby trigger a by-election? The Lib Dems should carefully consider this option. If their popularity will sink even further before the general election, then they should choose to have a by-election as soon as possible while there is still support for them in Bath. Alternatively, if they believe that they can solve their internal strife rapidly, and regain some trust from the electorate, then they should hang on until the general election. Calling a by-election would be a high risk strategy. A win in Bath, however narrow, would stabilise their decline nationally. Are they able to make a rational decision, and do they have the nerve to carry it through?

45. Are the Conservatives truly Eurosceptic?

To: North Somerset Times

Writing in the Daily Mail, Liam Fox MP has stated:

'Britain is lucky. We have a mainstream Eurosceptic party able to form a Government and offer a referendum. Only the Conservative party can do this. It is a tremendous responsibility and a phenomenal challenge. David Cameron will reap rewards if he seizes this historic opportunity.'

There are several problems with his assertion. Firstly, David Cameron can hardly be described as Eurosceptic. For example, he and Boris Johnson are both on record as strongly encouraging Turkey to join the EU. If he was Eurosceptic he would recognise that the expansionist EU has grown too large and cumbersome already. Furthermore, Mr Cameron has called for the EU to expand as far as the Urals, which is well inside Russian territory. He is playing with fire, and seems oblivious to the risks.

Secondly, the referendum proposed by the Conservatives is unlikely to happen. The suggestion that there would be fundamental changes in our relationship with the EU as suggested by Cameron is a fantasy. He is merely kicking the can down the road to the point where we will have limited ability to do so, short of exiting entirely, because the voting rules are changing to Qualified Majority Voting.

Thirdly, it is disingenuous to imply that UKIP is not mainstream. The party has decisively won a national election, has a rapidly growing membership, and is on course to take seats in Westminster.

46. Malaysian plane could have been spared

To: Western Daily Press

The tragic destruction of the Malaysian plane over eastern Ukraine could have been easily avoided using an inexpensive radio receiver and a laptop. Cheap digital TV dongles can pick up the data transmissions broadcast by aircraft which identify the flight name and aircraft location, using the ADS-B system. If only whoever had fired the missile had used this readily available equipment then they could easily have recognised it as a passenger plane. The lives of the 298 souls on board would have been spared.

It is my opinion that the world needs to have buffer states to act as intermediaries between superpowers. History shows us for example that as soon as Tibet was annexed by China, then conflict started between China and India.

For peace to be restored to Ukraine, I believe that the EU needs to back off from its ambition to encompass that territory. Russia also needs to let go, and leave Ukraine to develop in the way that the people of Ukraine wish. If Ukraine could develop as an independent, sovereign, and democratic nation, that would give us the best chance for peace. If it is absorbed partially or wholly into the EU then conflict between the EU and Russia is probable. Our armed forces have been scaled back due to spending restrictions, we are badly prepared to take on the Russian military machine.

References:
http://en.wikipedia.org/wiki/Automatic_dependent_surveillance-broadcast

http://www.theguardian.com/world/graphic/2014/jul/18/malaysia-mh17-flight-path-map-ukraine

47. Defection to UKIP

To: Somerset Guardian

'The emperor has no clothes'. This is effectively the message from Douglas Carswell MP on leaving the Conservatives to join UKIP. He said: "People have a right to expect a government that answers to Parliament, and a Parliament that's accountable to the people. ... His [Cameron's] advisers have made it clear that they seek a new deal that gives them just enough to persuade enough voters to vote to stay in [the EU]. It's not about change in our national interest. It's all about not changing things. Once I realised that, my position in the Conservative party became untenable."

It is refreshing to see an MP acting according to conscience and for the good of the country, rather than out of a misplaced loyalty to the Conservative party, which has changed considerably under David Cameron. The 'modern' Tory party has haemorrhaged traditional members whilst not gaining the support of progressive types – their strategy has failed. Cameron makes promises that he cannot keep. I am deeply suspicious of his promise to hold a referendum on our EU membership, Douglas Carswell has done us a huge favour by confirming that these doubts are valid. Before the 2010 general election Cameron promised to bring net migration down to a few 10s of thousands, and I believed him. It has gone up by 38% in a year. Cameron has fooled me once, he will not fool me twice.

Douglas Carswell is liked and respected in his constituency. He should retain most of the Conservative vote. He will also gain support from traditional Labour voters because uncontrolled immigration has had a serious downward pressure on wages and upward pressure on housing costs. Cameron tries to stitch us up, we can see that his promises are transparent and threadbare.

48. Jacob Rees-Mogg and UKIP

To: Somerset Guardian
To: Western Daily Press

I welcome much of the positive message regarding UKIP by MP Jacob Rees-Mogg in his article in the Daily Mail (7th September). However, it may be that Jacob finds UKIP to be perplexing. He suggests that Nigel Farage should become the future deputy Prime Minister. Nigel has made it clear that he is driven by the wish to do the best for our country, and not by personal ambition for political office or status.

In a way there is the analogy of the Temptations of Christ, who was taken up to the top of a mountain and offered the whole land as his kingdom. That temptation completely missed the point of his mission.

The Prime Minister has made repeated errors of judgement, over Libya, Syria, and Ukraine. He has failed to stand up to the Liberal 'Democrats', for example over boundary reforms which remain undemocratic. He may go down in history as the PM who facilitated the dissolution of the United Kingdom. Patriotic Conservatives cannot be happy with this record.

A number of members of the B&NES branch of UKIP have been in contact with Jacob for some time now, by letter and in person. We would very much like him to join us. As a patriotic gentleman I do believe that he would best serve the electorate of North-East Somerset from within UKIP rather than from within the Conservative Party.

References:
http://www.bristolpost.co.uk/UKIP-leader-Nigel-Farage-dismisses-pact-Tories/story-22889503-detail/story.html
http://www.westerndailypress.co.uk/Jacob-Rees-Mogg-calls-Conservatives-election-deal/story-22889337-detail/story.html

49. Is David Cameron truly Eurosceptic?

To: Somerset Guardian

I have a high regard for Jacob Rees-Mogg, he is concerned about the erosion of our democratic principles due to our membership of the EU. However I must question his statement that: 'David Cameron is undoubtedly the most Eurosceptic Conservative leader since Margaret Thatcher..'

It is incongruous to regard Mr Cameron as Eurosceptic in the context of his long-standing pledge to help Turkey to join the EU, and his more recent wish for the EU to extend as far as the Urals.

Turkey is slipping away from democratic principles. Dissent is treated harshly - internet freedoms are curbed, many journalists are in prison.

Of concern to the Conservatives may now be that, due to the constitutional crisis resulting from the vow to Scotland made my Messrs Clegg, Cameron and Miliband, there is a risk that there would be insufficient parliamentary time to implement the EU referendum bill. The electorate takes a dim view of broken promises.

References:
http://www.youtube.com/watch?v=vGqQoMyZMnA

http://www.independent.co.uk/news/uk/scottish-independence/scottish-independence-cameron-miliband-and-clegg-sign-devolution-vow-but-scots-sceptical-9736090.html

http://i4.dailyrecord.co.uk/incoming/article4265480.ece/alternates/s615b/1.jpg
http://www.express.co.uk/comment/expresscomment/486144/Conservatives-David-Cameron-EU-Referendum-Bill-Parliament-Debate

50. Bath the seat of the English parliament?

To: Bath Chronicle

If England is to have its own parliament, a good case can be made for it to be located in Bath. It certainly should not be co-located in Westminster because it needs to be a distinct entity from the proposed federal UK parliament. The idea proposed by David Cameron of English laws made only by English MPs is clearly a non-starter, because it is asymmetrical with Scotland, Wales, and Northern Ireland. It is transparently a party political ploy to advantage the Conservatives, and would at some point be overturned. He thinks he is being clever but he is not.

Winchester also has a good claim, because it was the principal location of the court of King Alfred (AD 849 – 889), and is the place where he was buried. However, although he was rightly called 'The Great', he was not the king of all England. The first king of all England, King Edgar was crowned on the site of Bath Abbey in AD 973. I believe that it is most appropriate, if we are to have an English parliament for it to be located in Bath.

Bath would benefit greatly from being the meeting place for the Members of the English Parliament (MEPs). Who knows, we may then dispense with the need for Members of the European Parliament. Surely there would be too many layers of government for efficient working?

References:
http://www.bathabbey.org/history

http://en.wikipedia.org/wiki/Alfred_the_Great

http://www.theguardian.com/politics/2014/sep/21/cameron-pressure-scotland-devolution-alexander

51. Labour Conference

To: Western Daily Press

Apart from some leg flashing by one of their 'apparat-chick' class warriors, the Labour Party conference has been deadly boring. Where are their bold new ideas, rather than re-hashed old ones? Where is their vision for the future? Where is their charisma? Where is their credibility on the economy? Or indeed the NHS – Labour PFI schemes are extremely expensive, no wonder NHS Trusts go bankrupt. Where indeed is their humility regarding their errors of judgement in towns such as Rotherham? It is a sad reflection on the poor quality of modern Labour that they very nearly trashed the 'Better Together' campaign, and had to wheel out Gordon Brown to save it and to save their party. He out-classed them all, Messrs Miliband, Darling, Alexander, and Murphy. And yet Gordon Brown ended his premiership in abject failure. How much worse a failure would Ed Miliband be? The quality of the conference message does not bode well.

Even so, it is possible that Labour may win the general election in 2015. If so, the Conservative would have to hold David Cameron to account for his repeated lack of judgement and common sense. For example he promised to bring net migration down to a few tens of thousands. He is an abject failure in this regard, which is an absolute gift to UKIP.

References:
http://www.dailymail.co.uk/debate/article-2765877/Labour-s-plan-force-employers-biased-against-middle-class-recruits-isn-t-just-lunacy-s-immoral.html
http://blogs.spectator.co.uk/isabel-hardman/2014/09/why-is-labours-shadow-cabinet-saying-so-little/

http://www.theguardian.com/uk-news/2014/aug/28/uk-net-migration-soars-to-243000-theresa-may
http://blogs.spectator.co.uk/coffeehouse/2014/09/the-simple-and-shocking-secret-to-the-working-class-vote/

52. Hinkley power station

To: Western Daily Press

'At last Hinkley gets EU backing' was the headline which grabbed my attention on Tuesday. It just seems unbelievable, doesn't it? Why on earth do we cow-tow to the EU on matters of strategic importance to our nation? Why on earth do we permit the tail to wag the dog? Why on earth did we, a once hugely successful independent nation permit ourselves to sink so low?

Whether or not you are in favour of nuclear power, you would have to agree that the decision whether to build it or not should rest solely with our own Government in Westminster, with our own democratically elected representatives and not in Brussels by people who we had never heard of, and who we cannot sack at the next election.

The GMB union welcomes the decision. Yet under the three terms of Labour Government, not a single new nuclear power station was started. The margin between generating capacity and peak demand is critically low. The Energy Minister under Labour was Ed Miliband. If we get electricity blackouts in the next few years we know who to blame!

It takes a decade to build a nuclear power station. By 2023 eight out of our current nine nuclear power stations will be shut down. By the end of 2015, 11.5 GW of coal and oil plant will have closed due to the EU Large Combustion Plant Directive. We were within six hours of running out of gas in March 2013. Summary: We are in a serious mess.

References:
http://www.westerndailypress.co.uk/Hinkley-nuclear-power-station-gets-ahead-UK/story-22963085-detail/story.html
http://www.dailymail.co.uk/news/article-1199129/Higher-energy-bills-inevitable-warns-Climate-Change-Secretary-Ed-Miliband.html
http://news.sky.com/story/1095134/gas-uk-was-six-hours-from-running-out

53. EU – complaint by Molly Scott Cato

To: Western Daily Press

The Green Party MEP Molly Scott Cato has complained about the lack of transparency within the EU decision making process, in this case relating to the Hinkley power station. Is she suggesting that the EU is corrupt and undemocratic?

It always surprises me that the Greens are pro-EU. If the UK is to have any hope of meeting our CO_2 reduction targets, then that cannot happen while the UK population is ever increasing. We cannot control immigration from Europe while we are in the EU, hence we have no control of UK population growth. Surely Ms Scott Cato has read the classic environmentalist book 'The Limits to Growth'?

References:

http://www.westerndailypress.co.uk/South-West-Green-MEP-Molly-Scott-Cato-shocked/story-22966873-detail/story.html

http://en.wikipedia.org/wiki/The_Limits_to_Growth

54. Headless chickens

To: Somerset Guardian

The headless chickens are coming home to roost! My mixed metaphor describes the mood at the Conservative Party conference. Yet another Tory MP has seen sense and defected to UKIP. Yet another statement of lack of faith in David Cameron has been spoken. The Tories are in panic, and are running around trying to offer gimmicks.

A well known local Conservative is apparently of the opinion that UKIP has only one policy. He has not been paying attention. UKIP has been hard at work developing a comprehensive, costed and independently audited suite of policies, covering defence, health, education, the economy, transport, agriculture, planning, law and order, communities and social cohesion, the commonwealth, etc. and of course on the EU and on immigration.

For the Tories to lose one MP is careless, but to lose two is Reckless!

References:

http://www.theguardian.com/politics/2014/aug/30/david-cameron-caught-virtues-vices-europe

http://www.telegraph.co.uk/comment/cartoon/

http://www.telegraph.co.uk/comment/11125001/The-Reckless-defection-is-a-test-of-Camerons-nerve.html

55. Subsidising solar farm

To: Bath Chronicle

What on earth are the Lib Dem councillors thinking? If the proposed Wilmington Farm solar array is a commercial enterprise then it should be costed at commercial rates and risk analysis, and they should obtain a bank loan on that basis. If it is to be a publicly funded scheme, then the council tax payers of B&NES need to have a direct say. The Lib Dems have created another fine mess, like the Dorchester Street bus gate.

Not everyone is in favour of solar farms. Some dislike the visual impact. I have two concerns: Firstly, that agricultural land is being used, which will result in more food being imported, putting up costs and CO_2 emissions required for transport. Solar farms are not as green as their advocates assume. Secondly, renewable energy is intermittent, and significantly more expensive than conventional power stations. People on limited income are struggling to pay for their electricity, they are subsidising wealthy land owners.

If solar panels were financially viable, then supermarkets and large retail outlets would have them on their roofs. The fact that they mostly do not is telling us something.

References:

http://www.bathchronicle.co.uk/Loan-500-000-Wilmington-Farm-solar-energy-scheme/story-22963177-detail/story.html

http://www.bathchronicle.co.uk/Drivers-caught-Dorchester-Street-bus-lane-fines/story-21033373-detail/story.html

http://www.energygrants.co.uk/solar_power/solar-pv-feed-in-tariffs.html?gclid=CI3st4zzhcECFQrjwgodAJ4AAw

http://en.wikipedia.org/wiki/Cost_of_electricity_by_source

56. The importance of being Johnson

To: Bristol Post

The two main political parties are struggling to make headway. The membership of the Conservative Party has about halved under David Cameron. Without an active grassroots support across the whole of the UK they are the walking dead, a collection of zombies even. No use blaming UKIP, their decline was well under way before UKIP became a force to be reckoned with. Labour has an even more significant problem at the moment – they picked the wrong Miliband! If he cannot remember important points such as the deficit or immigration when making an hour long speech, there really is no hope. Neither of them has had a proper job in the real world. How can Labour politicians expect to represent working people if they themselves have never actually worked?

Labour needs someone gritty and down to earth, they need to bring back Alan Johnson and ditch Mr Miliband. The Conservatives could also defenestrate Mr Cameron, he would have resigned anyway if Scotland had gone. Bring on Boris! Let us have some fun back in politics.

Johnson and Johnson oil is an emollient for babies. We need a political emollient for the whole of the UK, we are battered and bruised. UKIP is growing rapidly, the two main parties are on a slippery slope.

57. Theresa May – conference speech

To: Western Daily Press

Full of sound and fury, signifying nothing. The conference speech by the Home Secretary was full of passionate intensity, but is she correct? She quotes two paciferous verses from the Koran, unfortunately not in context, nor with any acknowledgement that they may have been abrogated (superseded). She echoes earlier speeches by David Cameron and Nick Clegg following the murder of Lee Rigby. She follows essentially the same script set by Tony Blair after the London bombings in 2005. Who do these modern politicians think they are kidding? We have the internet now, we can easily see through their smoke and mirrors. We need someone like Winston Churchill. He understood the existential threat building up in the 1930s. Few believed him, or wanted to acknowledge the painful truth. Or they tried to appease. We face another existential threat today. It is nearly a decade since the London bombings. Will we waste another decade listening to the heirs to Blair, while nothing substantial is done?

References:

http://blogs.spectator.co.uk/coffeehouse/2014/09/why-is-theresa-may-pretending-that-islam-is-a-religion-of-peace/

http://blogs.spectator.co.uk/coffeehouse/2014/09/theresa-mays-speech-on-terrorism-and-extremism-full-text-and-audio/

http://en.wikipedia.org/wiki/The_River_War

http://www.telegraph.co.uk/news/uknews/terrorism-in-the-uk/11133834/Lets-hear-it-for-Theresa-May-as-she-promises-to-silence-the-Islamists.html

http://www.theguardian.com/politics/2014/sep/30/theresa-may-tory-government-snoopers-charter

58. UKIP challenging Labour

To: Western Daily Press

UKIP is the main challenger to Labour in the Heywood and Middleton by-election. However it is a staunch Labour area, and it will be hard for UKIP to win. Nevertheless, there could be a way to achieve it.

The recent Survation poll shows the voting intentions with changes from the 2010 result: CON 13%(-14), LAB 50%(+10), LDEM 4%(-19), UKIP 31%(+28).

MP Jacob Rees-Mogg has repeatedly called for a pact between UKIP and the Conservatives. Naturally UKIP is skeptical about such a proposal. David Cameron has been thoroughly unpleasant towards UKIP. Mr Rees-Mogg could contact the Conservative candidate, to suggest he asks his voters to support UKIP instead. A defeat for Labour in their heartlands would greatly benefit the Conservatives at this time, delivering a psychological blow from which Labour would not easily recover before the general election.

This opinion poll already destroys the myth that a vote for UKIP is a vote for Labour. The Conservatives were never going to win it anyway. UKIP might just do so with a late surge, they are already ahead of where the Conservatives were in 2010, which was a disastrous year for Labour. 2015 could be a disaster for them too.

References:

http://survation.com/new-polling-for-the-heywood-middleton-byelection-survation-for-the-sun-data-tables/

59. No energy from Lib Dems

To: Bath Chronicle

At the Lib Dem conference the Minister for Energy and Climate Change Ed Davey gave a speech. It was telling that he completely failed to mention nuclear power, and yet this is the one 'grown up' source of energy which has low CO_2 emissions.

The EU is forcing us to shut down our coal power stations whilst inconsistently giving Germany permission to build new ones. We are getting inconsistent messages from the Lib Dems too. Ed Davey is in favour of fracking whilst the local Lib Dems are against. Whether you are for it or against it, the message is that you simply do not know what the Lib Dems truly stand for, or whether the local Party will be over-ruled from Westminster. The Green Party appears to be taking significant numbers of votes from the Lib Dems in B&NES. They were two percent ahead in the European elections in B&NES, and it would not be surprising if this gap widened further. At least you know where you are with the Greens and that they are consistent. They are already level with the Lib Dems on 7% in the latest national opinion poll, I foresee that this trend will continue, with the Lib Dems pushed into fifth place in the General Election. It is all about trust and credibility, the Lib Dems have lost it, and have run out of energy.

References:

http://www.prospectmagazine.co.uk/blogs/prospector-blog/energy-and-climate-change-secretary-ed-daveys-speech-to-the-liberal-democrat-conference

http://www.theguardian.com/environment/2014/aug/27/coal-power-stations-eu-emissions-target

http://theenergycollective.com/barrybrook/471651/catch-22-energy-storage

60. In B&NES – vote Labour get Tories

To: Somerset Guardian
To: Western Daily Press

There is a clear message from the Heywood and Middleton by election: the Conservatives are not at all serious about defeating Labour. If they were, and knowing that their candidate had absolutely no chance of winning, they should have stood down their candidate and given UKIP a clear run. UKIP would have easily won of course, but Labour would have been one seat further away from victory in 2015. Why cannot the Conservatives see it? There is no need for them to set up a complicated pact with UKIP, they simply need to avoid getting in the way.

The converse applies in B&NES. In the European election in B&NES Labour was behind the Greens, and a long way behind UKIP and the Conservatives, who were well in front with nearly the same number of votes as each other.   If you usually vote for Labour, you will need to vote for UKIP if you do not want the Tories. Labour should stand down their two candidates here, or else risk a Conservative government in 2015.

References:

http://www.theguardian.com/politics/2014/oct/11/nigel-farage-rules-out-ukip-election-pact-tories

http://www.dailymail.co.uk/news/article-2789512/record-poll-surge-gives-ukip-25-survey-hand-farage-astonishing-128-mps-puts-ed-miliband-new-low.html

http://www.theguardian.com/politics/2014/oct/10/labour-scrapes-byelection-victory-ukip-heywood-middleton

European election 2014 results for Bath & North East Somerset:

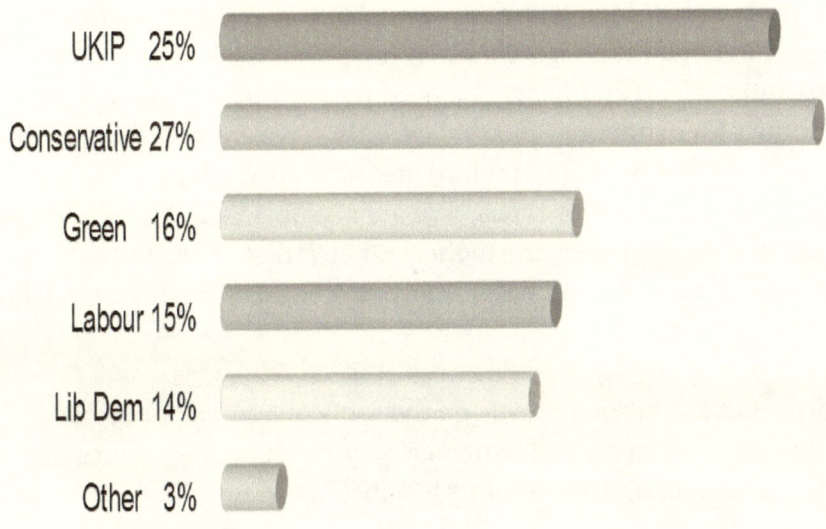

61. Subsidising solar farm - response

To: Bath Chronicle

I thank Cllr Paul Crossley for responding to my letter regarding the proposed Wilmington solar farm. However, I feel that his reply did not address my concerns regarding the loss of agricultural land and hence the need for increased food imports and therefore adding to food miles, or that we are all paying more for electricity as solar (and wind) are more costly than conventional generator types. We are all subsidising them, the more of them there are, the higher our electricity bills will be, and also the higher our food bills. Many people are struggling already to pay their bills.

I do not object to solar panels on the roofs of houses or business premises, provided that the owners pay for them themselves without expecting the rest of us to subsidise them.

It is surprising that the B&NES Conservatives support solar farms. They oppose house building on greenbelt, I thought they wanted to protect rural England. There is an apparent inconsistency which they need to explain.

Anybody who is concerned about the cheap, risky loan by B&NES Council to the Wilmington solar farm, or about the other proposed solar farms in our area can contact me via the North East Somerset UKIP website, www.nesukip.org.uk I want to see our green and pleasant land protected, not spoiled at local taxpayer's expense.

References:

http://www.bathnes-conservatives.com/questions-raised-over-councils-0-5-million-loan-to-solar-farm/

http://www.bathnes-conservatives.com/bnes-urged-to-go-further-inprotecting-greenbelt-sites-in-housing-plan/#more-1706

http://www.bathchronicle.co.uk/Loan-500-000-Wilmington-Farm-solar-energy-scheme/story-22963177-detail/story.html

http://www.energygrants.co.uk/solar_power/solar-pv-feed-in-tariffs.html?gclid=CI3st4zzhcECFQrjwgodAJ4AAw

http://en.wikipedia.org/wiki/Cost_of_electricity_by_source

62. Labour on the NHS (Draft copy)

To: Somerset Guardian

I have to reply to the misconceptions in the letter by Councillor Eleanor Jackson. It was Tony Blair who has saddled the NHS with the extortionate PFI (PRIVATE Finance Initiative) schemes. No wonder that most NHS Trusts are in the red. UKIP aims to reverse the PFI schemes.

Regarding her points about the downward pressure on wages. It is very simple, there is an over supply of cheap workers due to our open borders with Europe. Gordon Brown had no answer to Mrs Gillian Duffy when she raised her concerns, and Ed Miliband has no effective solution either. Labour has betrayed their core voters.

As demonstrated in the May elections, in B&NES UKIP is the only credible contender against the Tories. Labour has no chance of winning in Bath. In North East Somerset, if you vote Labour you will get the Tories.

References:

http://www.telegraph.co.uk/news/election-2010/7646088/General-Election-2010-Gordon-Brown-versus-Gillian-Duffy-transcript-in-full.html

http://www.theguardian.com/politics/2014/oct/11/nigel-farage-rules-out-ukip-election-pact-tories

http://www.dailymail.co.uk/news/article-2789512/record-poll-surge-gives-ukip-25-survey-hand-farage-astonishing-128-mps-puts-ed-miliband-new-low.html

http://www.theguardian.com/politics/2014/oct/10/labour-scrapes-byelection-victory-ukip-heywood-middleton

63. What a choice!

To: Bristol Post

What a choice we have in 2015. Will it be Ed Miliband or will it be David Cameron for PM?
One is the son of a Marxist, the other is a Groucho Marxist: "Those are my principles, and if you don't like them... well, I have others." As for Nick Clegg and his sorry excuses, his recursive promise breaking and lack of coherence has led to his party being in fifth place in a recent opinion poll, behind the Greens.

You can understand why the Conservatives would want to flood the country with cheap workers, it pushes up house prices, and gives them cheap plumbers and cheap nannies, but why on earth would Labour do so? It betrays their traditional voters by suppressing wages, increases rents, destroys quality of life. The new votes gained do not compensate for the traditional votes lost. This has puzzled me for some time, I now have a theory for it:

Labour thrives on grievances and on a sense of impotence. They need to perpetuate despair and poverty in order to give their party an apparent purpose. Social dislocation is their means of production of desperation. In 2004 they opened the borders to eastern Europe, with the promise that only a few thousand would come. They lied. My theory is that Labour wishes to create the conditions for a Marxist revolution. They are playing the long game, anybody who questions it are denounced as bigots.

References:

http://www.telegraph.co.uk/news/politics/labour/10837206/Labour-needs-a-straight-talking-pint-drinking-man-says-Gillian-Duffy.html

http://www.breitbart.com/Breitbart-London/2014/05/16/Labour-Candidate-Accused-of-Intimidating-Woman-into-Filling-Out-Postal-Vote

64. Labour on the NHS

To: Somerset Guardian

I have to reply to the misconceptions in the letter by Councillor Eleanor Jackson. It was Tony Blair who has saddled the NHS with the extortionate PFI (PRIVATE Finance Initiative) schemes. No wonder that so many NHS Trusts are in the red. UKIP aims to reverse the PFI schemes.

Given the disastrous outcomes for far too many patients in Wales, due to the poor state of the Labour run NHS there, it really is beyond credibility that Labour would lecture other parties on this matter. It would be more helpful if Labour would acknowledge their past errors with humility, and demonstrate a change for the better, for the good of the NHS patients.

It is estimated that health tourism costs the NHS around £2 billion annually. How can it be right that a British subject who has paid tax all their life has their treatment denied or restricted in order to pay for someone who has arrived in the UK without health insurance, has contributed nothing, and expects us all to pay? What does Cllr Jackson say to that?

References:
http://democracy.bathnes.gov.uk/mgUserInfo.aspx?UID=266

http://www.ukip.org/policies_for_people

http://www.dailymail.co.uk/news/article-2799411/labour-s-nhs-shame-exposed-mail-investigation-reveals-meltdown-labour-run-welsh-nhs-police-probing-allegations-horrifying-neglect.html

http://www.dailymail.co.uk/news/article-2470994/TRUE-cost-health-tourism-Foreigners-cost-NHS-2BN-year.html

http://www.theguardian.com/society/2014/sep/15/nhs-financial-crisis-deficit-1bn-hospitals

65. UKIP could win in Bath

To: Bath Chronicle

'Whatever you can do, or dream you can do, begin it. Boldness has genius, power, and magic in it!' - Goethe

On Saturday I and fifteen UKIP colleagues were canvassing and delivering leaflets in Larkhall. The response was remarkably good. We are gaining support from disillusioned Labour voters as well as those who want a change from the Conservatives and Lib Dems. The Greens seem to be gaining support at the expense of the Lib Dems. I very much have the feeling now that UKIP can win in Bath. The respected MP Don Foster will be retiring, the Lib Dems are losing the incumbency factor. Put it like this, in Bath, if you do not want the Tories to win then vote for UKIP.

A recent opinion poll published in the Guardian showed that when asked to respond to the statement "I would vote for UKIP if I thought they could win in the constituency I live in", 31% of voters said they agreed. This would be sufficient to win in Bath given the likely split of the vote. UKIP has the dream and the boldness, let us create some magic too!

References:

http://www.theguardian.com/politics/2014/oct/25/nearly-third-of-voters-prepared-to-support-ukip?CMP=twt_gu

66. Refund from the EU?

To: The Daily Telegraph

Sir,
If the lucrative exploitation of girls in Rochdale, Oldham, Rotherham, Telford, Oxford, Derby, and elsewhere can be stopped, can we expect a refund from the EU next year?

67. Incoherent Clegg

To: Western Daily Press

The Liberal so called 'Democrats' are a peculiar bunch aren't they? For a party with 'Democrat' in its name it appears hell bent on denying the very principles of democracy. For example they blocked the reform of parliamentary constituency boundaries. The current system favours one party over another, I would prefer to see the playing field as level as possible so that the democratic will of the electorate is properly and fairly expressed. I notice that Labour are not complaining, the field slopes in their favour.

Nick Clegg also campaigned for an in/out referendum on our EU membership in 2008. As soon as he gained power in 2010 his former zeal for democracy evaporated.

The latest indication of their poverty of principles is that Mr Clegg is extolling the virtues of his party not standing a candidate in the PCC (Police and Crime Commissioner) by-election in South Yorkshire. UKIP has a good chance of winning this election. It is simply bizarre that Mr Clegg now does not agree with the PCC system itself, which he jointly set up. The coalition agreement set out that: 'We will introduce measures to make the police more accountable through oversight by a directly elected individual, who will be subject to strict checks and balances by locally elected representatives...'

For the Deputy Prime Minister to not even bother to vote sets a poor example. I look forward to the day that Nick Clegg leaves the Lib 'Dems'. Maybe he could start a new political party with Russell Brand, at least he could be honestly anti-democratic then!

References:
http://www.libdemvoice.org/nick-clegg-im-not-voting-in-this-thursdays-pcc-byelection-43107.html#comment-322959
http://www.ukip.org/help_the_south_yorkshire_pcc_election_campaign

68. The divided Labour Party

To: Somerset Guardian

The Labour Party is divided by forces outside its control, and by its own self-inflicted incoherence. Ed Miliband is a symptom rather than a cause of its woes. It would not matter who replaces him if the root causes are not addressed, the successor would be struggling too.

Tony Blair has recently stated that it is not his role to save Labour – a bit rich, as it was he who abandoned their core working class voters, such as Mrs Gillian Duffy, for whom insult was added to injury by Gordon Brown. Her 'crime' was to raise the issue of excessive immigration into her home town Rochdale.

Labour is divided by its need to pander to contradictory special interest groups. It is losing votes and donations from the Jewish community because of its support for the creation of a Palestinian state. The demographic trajectory means that it must chase the Muslim votes, even if that means abandoning its long-standing Jewish support base, abandoning feminism, and abandoning its traditional core voters such as Mrs Duffy. Labour introduced Sharia Courts into the UK in 2008.

I believe we must have one law for all, with laws created in our own parliament by our elected representatives. Is this a bit radical? The Labour Party appears to have no idea how to run itself, how can it hope to run the whole country?

References:

http://www.dailymail.co.uk/news/article-2643397/Gillian-Duffy-IS-bigot-Senior-Labour-MP-triggers-new-immigration-row-saying-Gordon-Brown-right-rail-against-voter-famously-challenged-him.html

http://www.onelawforall.org.uk/

http://www.telegraph.co.uk/news/politics/ed-miliband/11223773/Tony-Blair-Its-not-my-job-to-save-the-Labour-party-any-more.html

http://www.independent.co.uk/news/uk/politics/palestinian-statehood-ed-miliband-says-labour-mps-must-vote-to-recognise-palestine-or-stay-away-from-parliament-9789946.html

http://www.timesofisrael.com/jewish-donors-said-abandoning-uks-pro-palestine-miliband/

69. Lies, damned lies and opinion polls

To: Western Daily Press

There is something seriously wrong with the accuracy of opinion polls when it comes to UKIP. The polls are simply not matching reality. For example an opinion poll conducted before the Heywood and Middleton by-election indicated that Labour were ahead of UKIP by nineteen percentage points. The reality was that UKIP came within a whisker of winning.

What is going wrong with the polls? It seems to me that part of the problem is the way that the voting intentions question is asked. It is usually asked in two stages, firstly "Would you vote for Conservatives, Labour, Lib Dems or others?" Then UKIP is listed in the second question. It is not surprising that when this form of question is used, UKIP is indicated having lower support than is true in reality.

A recent opinion poll using the two stage questions shows UKIP on 17%. A different poll which included UKIP in the first question shows UKIP on 24%. From this I think we need to always add six or seven percentage points to the headline poll rating for UKIP, unless the pollsters start asking a more balanced question.

Another poll, which I do believe based on what I hear when canvassing, is that if voters believe that UKIP can win in their constituency, then the support is at 31%. UKIP can indeed win many seats in the general election. If we will just believe, then we can move mountains!

References:
http://www.ukip.org/latest_poll_shows_ukip_on_24_demonstrating_other_pollsters_should_move_with_the_times

http://www.cityam.com/1414359100/poll-ukip-could-win-third-voters-2015

70. A debate please between Labour and UKIP

To: Western Daily Press

In the run up to the EU election in May, Labour showed a party political broadcast of Nick Clegg shrinking. Indeed the Lib Dems then lost all but one of their MEPs. However, what was noticeable for those looking out for such things, Labour completely failed to state what their own policy on the EU actually was. Did they want to be in or out? The silence was deafening. They left it to the Lib Dems to suffer the brunt of the UKIP onslaught.

Now Labour has woken up to the serious threat that UKIP poses to them, and Ed Miliband has responded by saying: "Others say the problem is the European Union and the answer is to leave that.... These voices are loud and insistent. But they are dead wrong. And need to be taken on."

This is fighting talk, the gauntlet has been thrown down. I am sure that Nigel Farage would be delighted to take on Ed Miliband, one to one, in a TV debate on our membership of the EU. It would be a high risk strategy for Mr Miliband, however if he could land a few punches on Mr Farage, it would do wonders for his own standing, and could turn around the prospects for Labour. Having all but made the challenge to UKIP, to back out now would be a sign of cowardice and will surely doom Labour anyway. The Tories have lost many voters to UKIP, Labour are losing them increasingly now also. Will they give up without a fight?

References:

http://press.labour.org.uk/post/102276146664/ed-milibands-speech-to-the-cbi

71. Some agreement with Conservative and Labour

To: Somerset Guardian

Last week's Somerset Guardian had two items from Conservative and Labour contributors which I agree with!

Firstly, MP Jacob Rees-Mogg described how Parliament was misled into thinking that it would have a say over the European Arrest Warrant. It seems to me that the Conservative backbenchers have been betrayed by David Cameron, the whole idea that Mr Cameron wishes to negotiate with the EU has been demonstrated to be farcical and non-credible. We risk losing the important principle of habeas corpus. Jacob shares this concern, he would find a warm welcome in UKIP. I hope that he will follow the principled actions of Messrs Reckless and Carswell, 'modern' Conservatives betray us all.

Secondly I can fully understand the annoyance of local Labour Party members that a Lib Dem is claiming credit for the support of Children's Centres in B&NES. Credit where it is due, the campaign has been primarily a Labour initiative. I spoke in support of the Bath Child Contact Centre at the Council meeting on the 16th January. B&NES Council had stopped the grant of £8,500. In context, this is about the cost of one and a half benches outside the Guildhall.

It is absolutely shameful that one in five children are living in poverty in Bath. I attended a meeting in Radstock recently regarding the Wilmington solar farm. I put the point that the more solar farms there are, the higher our electricity bills will be due to the green subsidies, and this impacts most severely on those struggling on limited incomes. Councillor Liz Hardman was in the audience, my point did not appear to dampen her enthusiasm for the solar farm. Labour needs to clarify their position on green subsidies and fuel poverty. Their current stance is incoherent.

References:

http://www.somersetguardian.co.uk/Claiming-credit-s/story-24524222-detail/story.html

http://www.somersetguardian.co.uk/Anger-Lib-Dem-s-claims-saved-children-s-centre/story-24524859-detail/story.html

http://www.somersetguardian.co.uk/B-NES-Council-chairman-switches-Labour-Lib-Dems/story-21255932-detail/story.html

http://www.jacobreesmogg.com/newspaper-articles/

72. Misrepresented by Labour

To: Western Daily Press

The former Labour MP for Medway, Bob Marshall-Andrews has caricatured UKIP as anti-immigrant. This is simply not true, he should be ashamed of spreading false allegations. UKIP is opposed to uncontrolled immigration, which is happening because we are in the EU. Over 500 million people have the right to come here if they want to. We have lost our sovereignty in our own country.

UKIP would put in place a border control system similar to that which Australia operates. Only those who would make a positive contribution would be allowed in, in sensible numbers, not heath tourists, benefit scroungers, or those who would undermine wages for the less well off and are a drain on the economy. Excessive immigration is putting severe strains on schools, hospitals, housing and infrastructure. Money spent on these means less money invested in technological innovation and scientific progress, necessary for a thriving economy. No wonder we are stagnating and in severe debt.

The electorate is far from stupid, the more that Labour misrepresents UKIP, the more votes UKIP gains at Labour's expense, because Labour is seen as desperate and deceitful. It is Labour Party MPs and ex-MPs who are not coherent or credible.

References:
http://www.theguardian.com/politics/2014/nov/17/ex-labour-mp-ukip-nasty-anti-immigrant-rightwing-tactics

http://en.wikipedia.org/wiki/Robert_Solow

Using his model, Solow calculated that about four-fifths of the growth in US output per worker was attributable to technical progress.

http://en.wikipedia.org/wiki/Solow–Swan_model

73. Intolerable fanatics

To: Western Daily Press

I am reminded of the scene from 'The Life of Brian' in which a man has been accused of blasphemy for the crime of uttering the word 'Jehovah'. He is facing the punishment by stoning squad, and uses the word again. The officiating priest tells him to "shut up, you are only making it worse for yourself" when the accused uses the word again. In the politically correct world which we now inhabit, I very much doubt that 'The Life of Brian' would be filmed today, and certainly not if there was any whiff of criticism of a religion with a shorter fuse than Christianity. Those who criticise a space scientist for wearing a shirt showing women in a style similar to Art Nouveau seem remarkably silent regarding the sexual exploitation of girls in Rotherham and Oxford. I like Art Nouveau, it looks like a perfectly fine shirt to me.

Interestingly, the punishment of lapidation for adultery does not appear in the Koran, only in the Hadith. There are plenty of other severe punishments mandated in the Koran.

Punishments for blasphemy still exist in the world today. Unbelievable! Do they know it is the 21st century not the 7th century? We should stop giving foreign aid to those countries, in my opinion. It only encourages them.

There will be a protest outside 10 Downing Street, 11am-1pm, 22 November 2014. To force HM Government to pressure Pakistan to end their blasphemy laws. We have to continue the pressure to release Asia Bibi, convicted and awaiting death for blasphemy. The life of a Christian mother of five children is at stake. Time to make a stand, while we still can.

References:
https://www.youtube.com/watch?v=bDe9msExUK8

http://en.wikipedia.org/wiki/Islam_and_blasphemy

http://en.wikipedia.org/wiki/Asia_Bibi_blasphemy_case

http://www.christianpost.com/news/christian-professor-arrested-for-blasphemy-in-pakistan-charged-with-same-offense-as-mother-of-five-asia-bibi-129854/

https://www.youtube.com/watch?v=bDe9msExUK8
http://www.theguardian.com/fashion/2014/nov/12/rosetta-scientist-shirt-women-twitter

74. Reckless wins

To: Western Daily Press

"The radical tradition, which has stood and spoken for the working class, has found a new home in UKIP." Mark Reckless said during his acceptance speech. Indeed an increasing number of former Labour voters are turning to UKIP, feeling that they have been misled and betrayed by the party which should have been working for their best interests.

This is the 271st target seat for UKIP, in other words nearly half of constituencies are at risk from UKIP. Nigel Farage said: "Looking forward to next year's general election, all bets are off, the whole thing's up in the air."

Of note also is that the support for the Lib Dems has collapsed, the Green Party achieved nearly five times the votes of the Lib Dems. This has obvious implications for areas such as B&NES, where the Greens beat the Lib Dems and Labour in the EU election in May.

References:

http://www.bbc.co.uk/news/uk-politics-30140747

75. A two horse race

To: Bath Chronicle

Whilst all the focus was on UKIP in the Rochester and Strood by-election, it was a significant event for other parties too. Notably the Liberal Democrats achieved less than one percent, a seventeenth of their previous result there. It was their eleventh lost deposit, and was their worst ever Parliamentary by-election result, they were only slightly ahead of the Monster Raving Loonies.

What are the lessons for Bath? MP Don Foster will be retiring, so they have lost the important incumbency factor. The Green Party is also eating into their vote. The Greens leapt up to sixteen percent in the EU election in B&NES. They are unlikely to win the seat, but are putting in the effort and thereby will collapse the Lib Dem vote. It looks as though Bath will be a two horse race between the Conservatives and UKIP.

References:

http://www.libdemvoice.org/rochester-strood-byelection-ukip-win-lib-dems-lose-11th-deposit-43449.html

76. Flags

To: Somerset Guardian

The Labour Party has a problem with flags. The recent tweet by Labour MP Emily Thornberry has shown how out of touch they have become. What is wrong with someone supporting the England team by flying our national flag?

I am reminded of all the fuss last year, when the Radstock town council stopped flying the flag of St George.

Councillor Eleanor Jackson (Lab, Radstock), said its use during the Crusades of the 11th, 12th and 13th centuries could mean the English national flag could be seen by some as offensive.

A spokeswoman for the Muslim Council of Britain, said it encouraged the flying of the St George's flag. She said: "St George needs to take his rightful place as a national symbol of inclusivity rather than a symbol of hatred. St George actually lived before the birth of Islam and should not be associated with any hatred of Muslims."

The Labour Party seems to be saying that ethnic minorities cannot be patriotic too. I do not agree with Labour, their stance is of course complete nonsense.

References:

http://www.theguardian.com/politics/2014/nov/23/emily-thornberry-damaged-labour-election-prospects-rochester-tweet

http://www.somersetguardian.co.uk/St-George-s-flag-Radstock-amid-concern-offence/story-19003959-detail/story.html

http://www.somersetguardian.co.uk/Demonstrators-fly-flag/story-19068349-detail/story.html

77. Do the Lib Dems believe in Democracy?

To: Western Daily Press

The evidence points to the uncomfortable truth that the Liberal so called Democrats do not believe in Democracy itself. For example they blocked the reform of parliamentary constituency boundaries. The current system does not give a level playing field, the democratic will of the electorate is not properly and fairly expressed. The rotten boroughs in the EU are even more noticeable, one vote in Malta for example is worth ten in the UK, and yet the Lib 'Dems' think the EU is wonderful!

Nick Clegg also campaigned for an in/out referendum on our EU membership in 2008. As soon as he gained power in 2010 his former zeal for democracy evaporated. We cannot now believe anything that he says. The mistrust works both ways – he does not trust the electorate to give the answer he wants, so he has done everything possible to prevent the electorate from being asked.

The voters in Rochester and Strood have given less than one percent of votes to the Lib Dems, a seventeenth of their previous votes and their eleventh lost deposit since 2010. It was their worst ever Parliamentary result - they only just beat the Monster Raving Loonies.

Before he became Deputy Prime Minister, Mr Clegg gave a rather peculiar interview with Andrew Marr in which he said immigrants should be prevented from moving to the South East of England. How would that work? Border posts across Hampshire? The voters of the South East have given their verdict on the incoherent nonsense coming from the Lib Dems, I hope that the Liberal 'Democrats' will soon be booted out of the South West too.

References:

http://news.bbc.co.uk/1/hi/8464064.stm

http://news.bbc.co.uk/1/hi/uk_politics/8468579.stm

ANDREW MARR:

On the same subject, what about the view that 160,000, 170,000 people coming in a year is unsustainable: it takes us to 70 million people before too long in this country and that is simply too many and this is a crowded country? Do you think that there is merit in that argument?

NICK CLEGG:

I think some parts of the country, clearly we have a lot of pressure on public resources, on public services, even on water resources - in the South East, for instance. It's not the case in other parts of the country. The second thing I would say, which people too readily forget, is that even now, after the large amount of people who've come into Britain in recent years, there are more British people living and working abroad than there are non-British people living and working in this country. It is a two-way street.

ANDREW MARR:

Sure.

NICK CLEGG:

If we simply pull up the drawbridge from one day to the next, we might actually find that we get a less welcome reception in other countries too. So ...

ANDREW MARR:

(over) I'm interested because you mentioned it again, but slightly confused, about this idea as to whether you could have more immigration into the borders of Scotland as it were and yet stop people who've immigrated there coming to the South East of England. It doesn't seem to me to be plausible.

NICK CLEGG:

It is plausible; it works in other countries. We are now looking at the way that works in other countries. So, for instance, the …

ANDREW MARR:

(over) People would have to be tied to a particular postal code.

NICK CLEGG:

Well it's relatively easy when people register to work, that they do so with local authorities so that you know who is working where. So, for instance, if we have a shortage of labour - as we do quite often in the fruit and vegetable picking industries of Lincolnshire, for instance - why should we not allow people to do that work on a seasonal basis?

ANDREW MARR:

You could make sure they didn't then move to London?

NICK CLEGG:

You could easily do that as long as you make sure, as long as you make sure of course that they're doing so above board.

ANDREW MARR:

Have you discussed this with colleagues?

NICK CLEGG:

Yes, yes, absolutely. No, this is a policy we've been developing over a long period of time. But let me tell you, that will only work if you know who's coming into the country and who's going out.

ANDREW MARR:

Sure.

78. Fanaticism

To: Western Daily Press

Nearly thirty years ago I had a friend who happened to be of Pakistani origin. Out of the blue he told me that he could no longer be my friend, which puzzled me. Had I upset him or been unkind? No. The reason was that he had become more religiously observant. It still seemed odd, I was happy to continue to be friendly. It was the first time that I heard the name 'Muslim Brotherhood', I was ignorant – remember there was no Internet then to look things up.

I thought no more about it until years later in 2005 there were the London bombings. I took the time to read the Koran. I read the verse: 'do not take the Jews and Christians for your friends'. At last I understood why the friendship was broken off.

Lord Pearson, a UKIP peer, has been severely criticised recently for pointing out that the killers of Fusilier Lee Rigby quoted verses from the Koran. We must at least acknowledge what was going through the minds of the murderers, if we are to to avert such a tragedy again. David Cameron will have no chance of solving this if he starts from a politically expedient yet false premise. We need evidence based decision making.

In Britain today there are communities inhabiting parallel lives. How can our hand of friendship be reciprocated if their beliefs forbid it?

It is my own belief that we must have one law for everybody, with everybody subject to the same law. The laws to be made by our elected representatives in our own parliament, not in Brussels, and not based on Sharia. That will at least give us a basis for a coherent nation, the current muddle of parallel laws serves nobody well at all.

References:

http://www.theguardian.com/politics/2014/nov/25/ukip-lord-pearson-quran-lee-rigby-murder

Pearson, who defected to Ukip from the Tories in 2004, took issue with David Cameron's statement that Rigby's murder was a betrayal of Islam and of Britain's Muslim communities.

He told peers: "My lords, are the government aware that Fusilier Rigby's murderers quoted 22 verses of the Qur'an to justify their atrocity? Therefore, is the prime minister accurate or helpful when he describes it as a betrayal of Islam? Since the vast majority of Muslims are our peace-loving friends, should we not encourage them to address the violence in the Qur'an – and indeed in the life and the example of Muhammad?"

http://www.thereligionofpeace.com/quran/009-friends-with-christians-jews.htm
Qur'an (5:51) - "O you who believe! do not take the Jews and the Christians for friends; they are friends of each other; and whoever amongst you takes them for a friend, then surely he is one of them; surely Allah does not guide the unjust people."

http://www.onelawforall.org.uk/

One Law for All
Campaign against Sharia law in Britain
Declaration

We, the undersigned individuals and organisations, call on the UK government to bring an end to the use and institutionalisation of Sharia and all religious laws and to guarantee equal citizenship rights for all.

Sharia law is discriminatory

Sharia Councils and Muslim Arbitration Tribunals are discriminatory, particularly against women and children, and in violation of universal human rights.

One law for all

Rights, justice, inclusion, equality and respect are for people, not beliefs. In a civil society, people must have full citizenship rights and equality under the law. Clearly, Sharia law contravenes fundamental human rights. In order to safeguard the rights and freedoms of all those living in Britain, there must be one secular law for all and no Sharia.

Petition

One Law for All

* We call on the UK government to recognise that Sharia and all religious laws are arbitrary and discriminatory against women and children in particular. Citizenship and human rights are non-negotiable.

* We demand an end to all Sharia courts and religious tribunals on the basis that they work against and not for equality and human rights.

* We demand that the law be amended so that all religious tribunals are banned from operating within and outside of the legal system.

79. Labour losing white van man

To: Western Daily Press

The tweeted photo of a white van and England flags has been a disaster for Labour. The YouGov opinion poll of Sun newspaper readers puts Labour firmly in third position behind the Conservatives and UKIP.

Another poll, which I do believe from what I hear when canvassing, is that if voters believe that UKIP can win in their constituency, then the support is at nearly a third of votes. UKIP can indeed win many seats in the general election. If we will just believe, then we can move mountains!

Opinion polls are significantly underestimating the true level of support for UKIP. A poll before the Heywood and Middleton by-election showed Labour were ahead by nineteen percentage points. In fact UKIP nearly won.

The problem is the way that the voting intentions question is asked. It is usually asked in two stages, firstly "Would you vote for Conservatives, Labour, Lib Dems or others?" Then UKIP is listed in the second question. When UKIP is included in the first question their true support is six or seven percentage points more. You need to add at least this number to the headline poll rating for UKIP, to get a true picture.

References:
http://www.express.co.uk/news/politics/541373/Support-for-Ukip-most-loyal-survey-found
http://www.express.co.uk/news/politics/539175/Boost-Farage-Ukip-second-Tories

http://www.ukip.org/latest_poll_shows_ukip_on_24_demonstrating_other_pollsters_should_move_with_the_times
http://www.cityam.com/1414359100/poll-ukip-could-win-third-voters-2015

80. Solar panels on roofs only

To: Bath Chronicle

I asked Molly Scott Cato a question at a public meeting in Bath before she became the Green Party MEP for our region: "Would it be better to put solar PV panels on roofs rather than on agricultural land?" She agreed with me.

My serious concern regarding solar farms is that we desperately need the land for growing food. It makes no sense even from an environmental perspective to import food many more miles than is necessary, and thereby expend even more CO_2. The UK population increased by nearly seven percent in a decade according to the census. The food imports will continue to increase, do we have the moral right to take ever more food from other countries? Many people are already starving worldwide, although with a higher percentage of CO_2 in the atmosphere plants do grow more rapidly.

If B&NES council insists on loaning half a million pounds of local taxpayer's money towards solar arrays, why not instead put the solar panels above car parks in B&NES? They would keep the cars cool in the summer and keep the snow and frost off in winter.

81. Democratic principles

To: Bristol Post

King Charles II made a declaration in 1660 regarding religious tolerance ensuring: 'a liberty of tender consciences, and that no man shall be disquieted or called in question for differences of opinion in matters of religion, which do not disturb the peace of the kingdom'.

We do today have parallel legal systems operating in the UK. In 2008 the Labour government officially introduced Sharia Councils, in order to make decisions on domestic disputes and financial matters, based on Islamic teachings. It does seem extraordinary that Labour introduced this, given that Sharia is discriminatory against women and non believers. I mistakenly thought that Labour was opposed to discrimination. This does indeed disturb the peace of the kingdom.

I also mistakenly thought that the Conservatives would return to having one law for everyone because their 2010 manifesto states that: 'Mending Britain's broken society will be a central aim of the next Conservative government.' Instead the Conservative led coalition has expanded the scope of Sharia Law by introducing Sharia Bonds - Sukuk - into the City of London. Anybody who has financial dealings with this might be subject to Sharia Law on our own soil, not English Common Law.

Today it feels rather radical to be asking for a return to true democracy, in which our laws are made in our own parliament by free men and women, not based on seventh century misogynist religious texts.

Prince Charles has long made it known that he wants the title 'Defender of Faith' rather than 'Defender of the [Christian] Faith'. He should be reminded that such an innovation risks the constitutional balance between the established Church, Parliament, and the Crown. He should take heed of his ancestral namesake.

References:
http://www.dailymail.co.uk/news/article-2853638/Koran-read-Prince-Charles-coronation-says-bishop-Critics-attack-proposal-accuse-Church-England-losing-confidence-traditions.html

http://www.secularism.org.uk/sharia-law.html

http://www.ddcap.co.uk/financial-secretary-sajid-javid-confirms-uk-debut-sovereign-sukuk-is-on-track-for-fy2014-launch/

http://www.breitbart.com/Breitbart-London/2014/05/29/Londons-Drive-to-Become-the-Sharia-Finance-Capitol-of-the-West

http://www.oxforddnb.com/templates/theme-print.jsp?articleid=92781

http://books.google.co.uk/books?
id=iZwhAQAAMAAJ&pg=PA394&lpg=PA394&dq=
%22Declaration+to+all+his+Loving+Subjects+of+the+Kingdom+of+Englan
d22&source=bl&ots=9_O0St3t1K&sig=OVrzRe4xPxDm7bpEmeN0K8u3B
3E&hl=en&sa=X&ei=Iut5VOm0No2u7AbmloDoBA&ved=0CCsQ6AEwB
Q#v=onepage&q=%22Declaration%20to%20all%20his%20Loving
%20Subjects%20of%20the%20Kingdom%20of%20England%22&f=false

http://www.theguardian.com/uk/2008/feb/07/religion.world

http://en.wikipedia.org/wiki/Muslim_Arbitration_Tribunal

http://www.dailymail.co.uk/news/article-2587215/Sharia-Law-enshrined-British-legal-lawyers-guidelines-drawing-documents-according-Islamic-rules.html